Christmas to the Max

Return to Welcome

Bonnie Edwards

Published by Bonnie Edwards, 2023.

CHRISTMAS TO THE MAX

First edition. January 10, 2023.

Copyright © 2023 Bonnie Edwards.

ISBN: 978-1989226100

Written by Bonnie Edwards.

Table of Contents

This book is dedicated to my brother Bob and my sister Jaunice. Gone, but loved always.

I'll see you both on the other side.

And for Ted, always.

What readers like you say about Christmas to the Max

5.0 out of 5 stars—Sweet second chance finding love and family... Reading this story made me curious to read the Welcome series. I read this book because I had to find out what happened to Max after meeting him in the Christmas Collection by this author.

5.0 out of 5 stars—Wow... once in a while I will pick up a romance novel. I'm glad I tried this one. The characters were well developed and the story has a good flow. I even got a little teary eyed at the end. Great story

5.0 out of 5 stars—Unexpectedly pleased beyond belief... I love anything to do with Christmas (& romance)—movies, books, music—all year long. I also enjoy love stories, & I thoroughly enjoyed this story of blending families!

5.0 out of 5 stars—Single Parents... This book was great! Ms. Edwards got the story right about single parents meeting, the challenges of dating & possibly merging 2 families. The situations were well depicted! As a former single parent who met another single parent, I could readily see that Ms. Edwards understood.

1

Chapter One

Late August, Welcome, WA

L	Max Whyte had been looking for a nice community to live in since June, when he'd announced his new position at a tech firm in Redmond WA to his daughters Lily and Willow. It was a big move to leave Vancouver Island in Canada and relocate across the border. But his ex-wife had done it, so he could, too.

The town of Welcome was perfectly situated. It meant a short drive south to Bellingham where his daughters now lived and an easy commute to Redmond for work.

Willow and Lily would start school in a few days. That would make seeing them in person difficult midweek. They'd taken to frequent video chats.

Lately, their chats had taken an odd turn as his daughters had fixated on his state of existence. He frowned as the conversation veered into his love life. Again.

"So, you're okay that mom married Cade?" Lily leaned into her screen as if Max might confess an undying, unrequited love for the woman who'd been more friend than lover.

"I'm more than okay, Lily. I'm very happy for her and for Cade."

"Okay, then." His youngest, at twelve, looked accepting. Then, in the next breath, she started with, "Now, we should find someone nice for you." She gave her older sister a look and it was Willow's turn to lean into the screen.

"Don't gang up on me," he said, knowing the plea would fall unheard. His daughters had selective hearing. Like most kids, he supposed.

He looked Willow in the eye, too. He'd tried to have a good thing with a woman a few months back, but circumstances between his kids and hers had come between them. To Willow and Lily, this break up looked like a challenge to get him to try again.

"Okay," Willow said with a sly look. "Don't worry. We'll find you the perfect woman."

"Yeah, and she'll be real pretty, too," Lily added. "We promise."

"Girls, I've got enough going on with my house hunt. I don't need a romance on top of settling into my new job."

"Have you seen any nice places this weekend?"

"Not yet. I want another fixer-upper like my last house. Tomorrow I'm seeing one near downtown. But I like Welcome so far. I'm sure you'll like it too." A typical American town, Welcome had a tidy main street that welcomed strolling.

The look that passed between his girls made a shiver go down his spine. Clearly, they'd soon be on the hunt for a suitable woman. Heaven help him.

Work. He needed to focus on his career and finding a new home; not on the lonely nights that closed in more tightly as he stared at turning forty in the new year. Aging had never been an issue before, but this year was a big one and the thought niggled. Forty and alone. He didn't need his children thinking the same thoughts.

"If we can find you a nice woman—"

"Stop right there," he interrupted Willow immediately. "No one needs to help me find a nice woman, least of all my children."

"The last one you liked wasn't very nice, so we thought since we picked Cade for Mom that you might want our opinion."

By tacit agreement, the adults had allowed the girls, both Cade's and Karyn's, to believe they'd done a great job matchmaking last Christmas Day. But Cade and Karyn had met months before, fallen in love and then parted because between them they had five daughters and couldn't see a way to blend their lives. Not with two full houses and an international border between them.

At Christmas, their five daughters had bridged the gap easily and opened the door to a future.

Max settled, content to let Willow and Lily chat about how nice Cade was and how adorable their new younger sisters were. He wondered if someday he'd find a woman they liked half as much as they liked Cade.

The next morning, Max drove along Main Street sucking up the quaint atmosphere.

When Max's house in Nanaimo on Vancouver Island had sold quickly, he'd decided he'd like another fixer-upper to work on.

Main Street in Welcome was small town America in every way. Each side provided angled parking for customers while most storefronts had apartments or offices on the upper floors. Welcome looked like a town full of regular people doing regular work. He saw a good mix of ages and ethnicities. If he'd read the sign right, a new subdivision was being built on the edge of town, but he wasn't interested in a new home.

Which brought him to the address he sought. One block along Main was Cross Street. He snorted as he realized Cross Street crossed Main and the intersection must have been the original four corners of Welcome.

Max was early for his appointment to see the home he was interested in, so he cruised past slowly, taking in the neighbors' places. Some were clearly owned by people who could no longer do their home maintenance or couldn't afford to hire landscapers. But some of the others had the stamp of new ownership. New paint, shutters, verandas, and sturdy new garages screamed new, young owners. He saw lots of potential on a street like this one.

At the end of the third block the street curved around a park. A half-empty parking lot beckoned so Max pulled in. Picnic benches followed the bend of the gently flowing river. He imagined the river flow would be more robust come the rainy season. He climbed out of his SUV to check out the park. He saw a riverside pathway meander down to where the house was. The path looked as if it went behind the house he would soon tour.

A playground full of children and parents sat to the right, away from the lure of the water. Children.

They'd become the bane of his existence. Any woman he dated who didn't have them, wanted them, and he already had Willow and Lily. More children were not on his agenda. He was too old to go back to having babies in his life. Forty loomed.

Forty and alone. He couldn't believe the alone part bothered him, but it did.

But if he couldn't see himself with babies, he sure as heck didn't want a woman with children already. After his experience with Lindy and her daughter, Izzy, last year he knew to steer clear of single mothers.

No way would he get involved with a woman with children. That left him with a mystery woman who needed to be happily child free for the rest of her life. And who wanted to be in his daughters' lives.

Not impossible. He snorted at the thought.

KAYLIN SIMPSON LOVED her twins. She truly, really, did. But some days she could scream until her throat collapsed and they wouldn't hear a thing. She'd thought two two-year-olds were hard. Having three-year-olds was a brand-new level of hell. They talked back, got stubborn, and were more curious. And taller, stronger, capable of climbing onto chairs and getting into cupboards.

And they were faster.

It was being faster that would kill her one day. Or them. Whatever. Someone would be dead.

Right now, Brody was telling a younger girl to go down the slide when she clearly didn't want to. The poor child looked scared and Brody yelling in her ear wasn't helping.

"Brody, please let the little girl take a breath so she's not so scared. And DON'T PUSH!" But he did, and Kaylin dashed for the end of the slide to catch the wailing child.

Too late, she realized she'd taken her other eye off Taylor. She scooped up the girl before she landed on the ground, and then spun her head to scan for her other boy.

There. By the swings. "Taylor! Stop right THERE!" But he didn't.

No, not her Taylor. He turned his head, glanced at her with a devilish grin and dashed for the road. *Chase.* He wanted to play chase.

In traffic.

Kaylin set the girl on her feet and ran after Taylor who'd already stepped onto the road. A car took the curve on Cross Street too quickly and Kaylin screamed her boy's name. Screamed it again. And again...

A man, tall, dark-haired, and with broad shoulders got there just before Taylor ran headlong into the car's path. Kaylin's heart stalled and her eyes stung.

Gasping for breath, she nearly collided with the big man who cradled her son in his arms, his large palm covering Taylor's head in a protective move. Taylor didn't seem to understand what had happened until he looked up into the stranger's face.

And screamed blue murder an inch from the man's nose.

Tires screeched as the driver slammed on the brakes. A woman opened the passenger side window. "Oh, my Lord! Did I hit him?" Her eyes were terror-filled, and her voice trembled.

The man shook his head and seemed to hold tighter to Taylor as he bent toward the opened car window. "No," he said. "But you took that curve pretty fast." He didn't yell it, the way Kaylin wanted to, but he got his point across.

The woman looked shaken and chastened. She eased the car to the curb and rested her head on the steering wheel. She'd been as badly shaken as Kaylin and the stranger.

A sudden screech from behind her had Kaylin spinning to see where it had come from. "Brody! Don't you dare!"

She snatched Taylor from the stranger's arms and lumbered under his weight back toward the swings where Brody was attempting to climb onto the big kids' swing. He'd been complaining for weeks about the baby swings and she wasn't sure how much longer he'd agree to use them.

She was still shaking over the miss with the car and wanted, more than anything, to get these boys out of this park and home where she could contain them.

If only she had the energy. She let Taylor slide to the ground and clasped his hand firmly as she walked the rest of the way toward the swing set. "We're going home," she announced in her most commanding tone, "as soon as I thank that man for saving Taylor's life."

Brody, for once, looked contrite. "I saw, Momma. He's over dere." And her boy pointed to a picnic bench that faced the river.

The man sat atop the table alone. His silhouette against the light showed broad shoulders that tapered to a trim waist. She already knew he could move like lightning when he needed to. His hair was trim on the sides but had some length on top. Odd that he'd be alone in a park on a lovely morning. Most people were jogging along the riverside trail or in the playpark like she'd been.

As she walked toward him, he pulled out his phone and started thumbing the screen as he scanned it. She hadn't seen him here before, and she recognized a lot of the regular park users.

She used to know people in Welcome when she was a kid. And he wasn't one of them, either.

Correction. Her aunt and uncle had known people here. She'd only been a summer visitor, so she'd been limited to playing with neighborhood children. Still, Welcome was where her most carefree memories rested. Even though her aunt and uncle had retired to Arizona, it was Welcome that had called to her when she'd needed to make a change in her life.

Returning to Welcome last month hadn't been as easy as she'd expected. Her business hadn't taken off the way she'd hoped, and daycare was more expensive than she'd planned for. She certainly could not take her kids to work. Construction sites were not safe for curious children.

Some of the people she remembered in Welcome gossiped and held grudges, but for the most part, people here were okay. Like this man who'd jumped into action for a total stranger. Gratitude made her heart lighter than it had been in weeks.

She had her boys safe and sound. That was what mattered.

"Hello," she said as she pulled alongside the picnic bench. Both boys for once, were silent, as the man raised his gaze to assess her.

"Yes?" He made a face as if she'd interrupted something important.

"I wanted to thank you for what you did. I'm still shaking and I'm sure I never would've got there in time." She'd been two steps away, but still, they were the longest two strides ever.

His gaze raked the twins and his eyebrows rose. "You've got your hands full, but next time keep a closer watch on them. I won't always be around for back-up."

Typical non-parent, always certain children could be corralled or held back or kept safe every second of every day and that they listened. *Hah*!

Kaylin backed up a step. "Sure, I'll keep a tighter grip. Maybe tether them to a stake in the ground. Keep them in the basement in cages, maybe. You've given me a lot to consider in regard to keeping my children safe." She raised her right eyebrow and glared at the know-it-all. "Thanks for that, too."

Chapter Two

Fifteen minutes after the feisty woman with the twins stalked off with them firmly in tow, Max climbed out of his car in front of the worn-out two-story Victorian that reminded him of the house he'd renovated in Nanaimo. The house before he'd completed his renovations.

He got a warm feeling as he gazed at the beauty of a fixer upper.

A family-sized minivan pulled up behind his SUV and a blond man climbed out. As he rounded the hood he spoke. "I'm Logan Hughes," he said. "You're here. Great."

Max recognized him from his website photo.

Logan stuck out his hand in welcome.

"Max Whyte," he said as he shook the real estate broker's hand.

"Any trouble finding the place?"

"None at all. I found the park at the end of the street, too." Max hooked his thumb to indicate the direction. "Glad to be here. Welcome seems like a nice town."

"It is. And this house is typical of the downtown area." Logan waved him toward the front walk. "In the early years Cross Street was where the area doctors, lawyers, and other well-to-do people lived."

Max nodded, thinking that a view of the river would have been a draw when the house was new. Maybe some of the homeowners had had a dock on the river. He couldn't wait to see what the view was today.

He followed the other man along the walkway. The wood on the steps bowed under their feet and then he found the veranda floor was no better.

"Spongey," he noted.

Logan nodded in agreement. "As I said on the phone, the place needs major renovations. But that's reflected in the price."

Max expected peeling paint and old wallpaper and his guess was confirmed when Logan opened the formerly elegant door. With an oval stained-glass window, the door looked original. Once inside he saw the wallpaper was solidly, undisputedly, 1970s.

"Older folks?" he guessed aloud.

"You got it in one. A couple raised their children here and now the granddaughter wants it sold. She's the only one who ever visited the widow and she inherited the property when Mrs. Jones passed."

Max nodded. "If there's only one heir then there won't be any family feuds over the offer." Siblings battling over a couple of thousand dollars could nix offers to purchase. Offers on real estate could fail, tainted by childhood baggage.

"The granddaughter is anxious to sell before the new school year," Logan explained. "She plans to quit her position at the elementary school and travel the world."

Max had never considered hitting the road that way. Walking away from his life wouldn't enter his head. He and Karyn had married and had their children early, exactly as they'd wanted. Best decision he'd ever made. But, he didn't want to make it again, he thought wryly.

By now he and Logan had wandered through the living room on the left and the dining room on the right. Both rooms had fireplaces, more for décor than any useful purpose in recent years. But the mantels were original and ornate. The mirrors in the centers were dark with age spots. Converting to natural gas would easily work.

The kitchen spanned the back of the house and Max was happy to see a gas stove that appeared to be a newer vintage than the old refrigerator. The fridge door had been left open and the cavity stuffed with newspapers. The carbon on the paper apparently filtered the smell.

"New appliances right away," Logan said with a grimace.

"No surprise." Max walked to the window that overlooked the backyard. "There's a tree down in the yard."

"Yes. It was hit by lightning in a storm last summer and Mrs. Jones was too ill to take care of it. The tree was old, and half rotted out, but it didn't hit anything when it fell."

And the granddaughter hadn't helped the old lady deal with the fallen tree.

"And that's the river I saw from the park up the street?" Beyond the rickety back fence water sparkled in the sun between the gold leaves. Once they fell, he'd have a clearer view.

He remembered the curve in the road by the park. "The riverside trail crosses the property?" A greenbelt of trees and shrubs shielded the back of the house from passersby. But again, the shield would be gone when the leaves fell.

"Yes, it's back there, beyond the trees," Logan explained. "The property is private, though. With the fence repaired, walkers won't see the yard."

Max thought of the pretty woman with curly brown hair and brown eyes. He wondered if she walked the twins along the trail. Her eyes had sparked when he'd prodded her about watching her boys. She'd tossed back a snarky comment and stomped off. He held back a grin at the memory. If she walked with them along the river, she likely had them within reach.

"Actually, the river widens at that point," Logan said with a sigh. "I've got to be honest. Sometimes locals swim there because it's shallow and slow. In summer, you'll hear kids in the distance. But mostly it's families, not rowdy teens." He cleared his throat. "I bring my own brood here when we can swing it."

"Brood?"

"My wife and I have five children. Her three and our own twins."

Logan Hughes was the father of those boys? He turned stiffly toward the other man. "I saw a woman with twins in the park earlier.

About three? Cute as hell. You're a lucky man." But his mind reeled at the thought of five children. He could barely keep up with his two. He had Lily and Willow part-time, but Karyn also had Cade's three daughters full-time. His head spun at the chaos these two families must live with.

"Nope, not ours," Logan was saying. "I've got a boy and girl with my wife and they're less than a year." The man's grin split wide and Max recognized fatherly pride.

He felt the same about Willow and Lily.

"I have two girls, twelve and fifteen turning thirty," Max said with a laugh. "They'll want to swim at the river bend too, so the sound of families having fun will not be a problem."

As long as that woman kept those boys tethered to a stake in the ground like she'd said, he'd be able to relax when he heard the screeches and laughter. "Let's head upstairs and we'll save the basement for last."

Logan clapped him on the back. "I'm glad the place hasn't scared you off. Yet," he joked.

An hour later, after a thorough walk-through, Max made his decision. "This is fast, but I recognize a diamond-in-the-rough when I see one." He mentioned his lowest offer and cited the expenses he'd be incurring for the work that had to be done while Logan nodded his agreement and understanding.

"I'll talk to Denise and see where she stands." Logan hesitated beside his minivan. "Out of curiosity, will you be doing most of the work yourself?"

"Mostly. I'll hire an electrician because these old places can be tricky. Can you recommend someone?"

"I can recommend a couple of different companies so you can make your choice."

"Thanks, I'll take you up on that."

"What about painting and decorating?"

"I might do it myself, depending on the time. I'd like most of this done by Christmas."

"Christmas? That's nearly impossible without a full crew."

"I know. The last place I owned took me most of a year." He scrubbed his hand across his jaw. "I'll think about hiring more people." He grinned. "But that may make for a lower offer when push comes to shove." He had drywall skills and decided he could handle the basement on his own.

"If you decide to hire, that woman with the twin boys is looking for work. She stopped by my office the other day to introduce herself." Logan raised his hands as if in surrender, then continued, "I can't say how she is to work with, but she was enthusiastic. I got the feeling she's having a hard time settling back into town. Not to mention being a woman in a building trade. Not the easiest thing to break into."

"She's new here?"

"She spent summers here as a kid and loved it. I believe she wants her boys to have the same kind of life."

Max made a non-committal sound. "That's commendable, but I need experienced people if I want this project to go smoothly." He mentally scaled back his expectations for completing the project. "I'll be happy if the girls' bedrooms and the kitchen are done by Christmas."

In his mind he saw a huge Christmas tree full of sparkly lights standing over a pile of wrapped presents in the living room. The golden glow from the miniature lights would give the tired walls a warm hue. Everything looked better with Christmas lights.

"Her name is Kaylin Simpson if you want to find her work online." Logan interrupted Max's thoughts. "She has a website and a profile on a job-seeking site." He shrugged as if it meant nothing to him if Max looked her up or not.

Employing Kaylin Simpson could mean trouble. She was interesting and Max found her appealing with her pretty face and tart tongue. But he'd never overstep employer-employee boundaries. He did not need to be in a want/can't have place. And he'd seen the messiness of workplace romance gone wrong.

Renovations and settling into a new town were challenge enough. He had to focus on those things, not on his empty bed.

If, in a few weeks, he wanted to spend time with Kaylin he'd ask her out; after she'd had time to forget his wisecrack about keeping her boys in hand. Her snarky response still brought a smile to mind.

He would *not* hire her. No way.

If Kaylin ever agreed to a date it would be because she wanted to spend time with him, too, not because she was his employee. That way they'd be on equal footing.

Logan cleared his throat, bringing Max back into the here and now. "We need to get this offer presented before anything else," Max said. "I'll follow you to your office and we'll get the paperwork done."

With a nod, Logan climbed into his minivan, all business.

Hughes Realty sat above the Welcome Bakery. Hughes ran a smaller operation than Max had expected. Two desks. The bakery scents from below made Max's stomach growl. "I expect you do a lot of work on the web and from your phone and tablet."

Logan gave him an honest smile and a light shrug. "The whole industry has shifted. Less face-to-face, more self-serve. Buyers look for properties online now. Which is a shame because places like the Jones house can be overlooked in the rush for new builds."

Max wandered to the window that overlooked Main Street. "Where do you live in town?" He asked this question of real estate professionals, the same way he asked car salespeople what they drove.

Logan chuckled. "Actually, we're living with extended family for now. We're renovating a big place two blocks from the house you want, so we'll be neighbors. We couldn't swing the riverfront, though. Too expensive with five children."

The answer was perfect. If Cross Street was good enough for Hughes, it would be good for Max, too. Willow and Lily would love having the river to swim in right behind the house. Maybe he'd install a gate for easy access.

With luck, he'd see Kaylin and her twins there occasionally. If he did, he could help her keep an eye on them.

"I'M GETTING MARRIED." The boys' father, Connor, whined in a way that Kaylin hoped Taylor and Brody would never hear. The sound grated on her eardrums although she was certain it was supposed to make her feel sympathy for his suffering. But whining about marriage was a new one. She gave him points for creativity.

"Married? You've never mentioned being serious with anyone." She should have expected this conversation with her ex to go sideways; they always did. Any day, she expected Connor to run out on them and be done with it.

"You heard me. A wedding's expensive. I can't afford to pay child support right now. Do you have any idea how much flowers cost? Never mind the rest of the crap."

Of course, she didn't. She'd never planned a wedding or been a bridesmaid.

Kaylin groped for the kitchen chair at her back and sank into it. "I'd have thought you'd have run out of excuses by now. But this one's fresh."

She closed her eyes and held in a groan of disgust. Pointing out Connor's failings as a man, a father, and a decent human being never got her anywhere so she swallowed the rest of her words.

The only thing that could make Connor pay on time was a lawyer and she couldn't afford the one she'd used before.

She couldn't afford anything right now. She'd be forced to go to legal aid. But that would take time she didn't have, so she sweetened her voice.

"Congratulations, Connor. But you must have something for your children." Her grip on the phone tightened. "By next week we'll be at a food bank."

"You should have thought of that before you moved up there." The punishing sneer in his voice made her stomach roll. Connor loved being right more than anything.

"Send a hundred dollars for groceries and I'll wait two months for the next support payment. I promise." Surely, she'd be working by then. Even if it were minimum wage, she'd take it. She'd do anything to keep her boys fed and happy.

Kaylin waited with her breath held.

"All right, I'll send it," he said, putting on a magnanimous voice. The roll in her stomach turned into a tidal wave.

She released her breath softly so he wouldn't hear that she'd been holding it. "That'll be fine. Send it today. They need milk. I'm almost out."

"Crap. How did you let things get this bad?"

"I didn't. You're the one who left, remember? Twins were too much, and you couldn't *deal*. I think that was the word you used." Too bad for him. Connor was missing out on the best experience life could bring.

"You'll have the money in an hour." He hung up, leaving her hanging on dead air. He hated having his shortcomings pointed out. Leaving a woman pregnant with twins and a dying mother was too ugly for Connor to accept about himself.

She shuddered at the memory of the day he told her he was leaving. She'd known it was coming, ever since she'd told him about her pregnancy. His response had been cool and detached as if he doubted what he was hearing.

But then, when her sonogram showed twins, Connor had lost his temper in front of the technician. He'd whined and for the first time she'd heard it. Until then, she'd ignored his wheedling tone when things weren't going his way. He'd turned sour as soon as they'd walked out of the clinic. Not only had she needed to process the idea of twins, but she had to face the loss of her relationship at the same time.

And then, she'd gone to the hospital to tell her mother the news. Not about Connor leaving, that would've been cruel under the circumstances, but about the joyous news of two grandbabies for her mother to love.

They'd both understood she wouldn't live long enough to see the babies, but it didn't matter. The joy in her mom's eyes had given Kaylin the strength to accept single parenthood without her mother knowing what Kaylin had to face.

So, how *had* she let things get this bad? By allowing Connor to skip months of payments whenever he made an excuse, that's how. A new car payment was more than he'd expected. Next, it was a move to a new apartment. And her favorite, a vacation that he badly needed. And now he expected her to let him skip another month because he was getting married.

She'd believe *that* when she met his new wife. Connor insisted marriage was too confining and he'd never shackle himself.

Her pregnancy had been a case of a broken condom while her body adjusted to new birth control. For that short time, she'd wanted to abstain, but Connor wouldn't hear of it. Too bad she hadn't seen the whining for what it was *before* she'd given in.

She'd hoped Connor would set aside his fear of commitment and accept being a father. But in the first weeks of her pregnancy her niggle of doubt grew to a certainty that he would not accept responsibility.

Conner Grimes had fooled her. She'd offered him her body and her heart. But he'd never wanted her in the first place. For three years, they'd seen each other weekly. Now, she understood the nights he wasn't with her, he was likely with someone else. She'd thought they were exclusive. He'd insisted, in fact, but she knew better.

And now, she'd enabled that loser to put her here, in a cheap basement apartment that was too small for her and her boys in a town that only seemed idyllic. She'd returned to Welcome because it was cheaper to live here than a bigger town and she'd hoped running her own renovations business would pave the way to better pay. She'd cossetted and enabled Connor this whole time.

No more.

She might be living broke, but she'd never be poor, not with Brody and Taylor to love. No, her life was full and sometimes it was hard to be alone, but it was her life and she faced her troubles head on. If she found decent paying work, Connor would be out of their lives forever.

The thought of him being gone brought a smile to her lips. And the smile brought a sliver of hope for her future here.

"Brody, Taylor, we're going for a walk this afternoon." They'd go along Cross Street and she'd look for work there.

"Okay. Then can we go to the park?"

"We may not have time. It depends if I start talking to people who want to hire me." She cut a peanut butter and jelly sandwich in half and handed the pieces to them. "You can share an apple when we go for our walk."

Soon, they'd hit another growth spurt and half a sandwich wouldn't be enough to keep them until dinner. She hoped the apple would help.

From the park earlier, she'd seen a couple of houses in need of repairs and she wanted to approach the homeowners. If she saw any renovations going on, she would talk to the contractors or the laborers. However she did it, she'd get work.

She had to. Connor's *generous* gift of one hundred dollars wouldn't go far.

What was it with men? This morning, that man in the park had ripped into her for Taylor's dash into the road as if she'd been negligent, and now Connor wanted to rub her face in it for returning to Welcome.

The man in the park had saved her boy, no doubt, but he hadn't seen her situation. In the moment, catching that little girl on the slide had been a priority. Seconds later, she'd been dashing across the grass with her heart in her throat.

Twins at three were a handful for two parents, never mind a single one. She huffed out her indignation. Connor and that man thought they knew everything. *Hah*! They didn't know a darned thing about her day-to-day existence.

Chapter Three

Three hours after seeing the house on Cross Street and four after saving Kaylin's boy's life, Max cruised along a country road heading toward Welcome. He'd criss-crossed the area and had enjoyed the drive. Happy with his decision on the house, he like the sight of rolling fields interspersed with stands of cedar and fir trees. This was a gently pretty part of Washington State.

The boy he'd snatched up had been cute as a cherub and twice as fast. He'd flown across the park from the swing set like he had wings on his feet. A quick glance had told Max nobody was trying to catch the little guy, so he'd loped a few feet closer, to be safe.

Then, a brown-haired beauty had taken off after the boy, but Max had seen a car coming into the curve. His lope had turned into a dash.

Just in time, he'd scooped up the kid. His chest clanked as he imagined for the hundredth time what could have happened. He grimaced at the memory.

He hadn't meant to snap at Kaylin, but leftover fright and adrenaline had made his tongue sharp. Twins. About three if he was any judge.

He'd decided hours ago that he wouldn't consider hiring Kaylin to help renovate the house, so he wasn't sure why he kept thinking about her big, soulful eyes and her wild mane of curls, but he kept replaying their meeting. He smiled in memory at her sharp tongue when he'd inadvertently stepped on her ego.

He shouldn't still be thinking about her, but he couldn't quit.

At the top of a slight rise in the road, a sign caught his eye. *Bowler's Rescue.* The sign had a picture of a cute dog swinging below it.

A dog. He hadn't had one since he was a kid. A lab cross, old Rex had been with him through skinned knees at ten and college heartbreak at twenty. It had killed him to see the old soldier pass away.

A pang near his heart highlighted his ancient grief. He'd loved that dog. And Rex had loved him. He wasn't sure why he hadn't brought home a pup for his daughters, but he and Karyn's lives had been a mad rush of activity. The timing never seemed right to bring a dog into the mix.

Idly, he wondered if Kaylin's twins had a dog. They were a good age to get one. At three, they could be taught to be gentle.

A memory of Rex filled his mind and somehow, the SUV, with an apparent will of its own, turned into a long, rutted gravel driveway.

He pulled to a stop alongside an older white bungalow with green trim, behind a late-model pickup truck. Max sat for a moment, hands on the steering wheel, wondering what he was doing here. *A dog?*

For months he'd been grousing about being alone when everyone around him had found a new love. His ex, her best friend, and even the best friend's daughter had recently married. The last couple of Christmas seasons had been about finding someone special.

Christmas. If you weren't surrounded by family, if you weren't wanted, it was a bleak time of year.

A new school year loomed, and his daily life would be about the renovations, but still he sat behind the wheel staring at the house, remembering Rex and thinking that Christmas would be on his doorstep in no time. He didn't have time for a pup, not with a new job, his daughters settling into a new home and family and an old house to fix up. Stupid idea. He waited for the urge to pass, ignoring the warm memories of his old buddy.

Christmas. His parents were making noises about having the girls visit them in Mexico again, but he figured Karyn and Cade would want them at home since it would be their first Christmas as a blended family. Also, Willow and Lily had both mentioned they'd like to be home this year. They needed to be here, not in Mexico. It would be impossible to have his home ready for guests by then so he couldn't invite his parents to come stay.

Christmas was about tradition and comfort and having the familiar. He wanted that for his girls.

Maybe it would be easier for them if he went to Mexico on his own and left Willow and Lily here to enjoy the holiday with their new sisters. No one needed him taking up space and butting into their new lives.

The idea chafed, but what the hell else could he do? Hang around like a barnacle on a barge, interrupting their family time? He couldn't see it.

In the distance, he heard a dog bark, then another and soon, a chorus. He lowered his window. Yips, bellows, and baying noises came from behind the white house. A cacophony of dog voices, all saying "come on back and check us out."

A retriever, he thought. A big dog. A man's dog. A German shepherd maybe. They were fluff balls as pups.

He shut off the ignition and climbed out of his vehicle as the front door of the house opened. A fifty-something woman with iron-grey hair and a questioning expression stood on the porch, eyeing him.

"Hello. I see you have a dog rescue."

"You have an appointment? Because I don't have anyone on the schedule." She squinted down at him.

Max shook his head. "Sorry, no." He ran his fingers through his hair. "I wouldn't mind taking a look, though."

"What for?"

"A dog," he said clearly. He almost said, "what else?" but thought better of it. This woman looked like she could send him on his way without a second thought. And suddenly, he wanted the soulful eyes of a dog looking at him every day. He wanted the uncomplicated affection of a dog. He wanted to walk one, play fetch with one, and talk to one.

Something of his thoughts must have shown on his face, because the woman descended the three steps and waved at him to follow her.

"I'm Karen Bowler and the dogs are this way. You'll need to fill out an application, of course and someone will stop by your place to see what kind of home you offer. We're careful here. Don't hand off dogs to strangers or people we don't know anything about." She gave him a sidelong glance.

"I got that," he muttered. He wouldn't be leaving with a dog today.

If he did snag a dog today, he'd be required to change suites in his hotel. Extra work and time on a busy day. Still, he felt sour about the delay.

"I'm moving to Welcome," he said to prove his good intentions. "My name's Max Whyte." He held out his hand, but she ignored the gesture.

"So Max Whyte is moving to Welcome. When?"

"I hope sooner than later. I put in an offer on a house and I'm killing time until I hear back. You've got a slice of heaven here in Welcome."

"We like to think so."

They walked to the area back of the house and he came to a dead stop. A pit bull ran toward them, eyes bright and interested. His tongue lolled out the side of his mouth and Max could swear he saw a smile.

"This is Beau," she said. "I tell people he's friendly."

She wanted him to feel intimidated. This was a test. He eyed the dog. Beau advanced toward him, his body language open and, indeed, friendly.

In his prime, the white and black dog had one black ear and eye and the other was white. His back had a black saddle and his black tail ended with a white tip. All in all, he was a handsome dog. A man's dog.

"Is he available?" There was something welcoming about Beau that Max responded to. And hell, yes, anyone could see he was friendly. He let Beau sniff his fingers then gave him a scratch behind the ears.

"No. He stays."

Okay.

"I might as well tell you right now, you're not walking out of here with a dog today."

"I figured," he said with a nod, already eyeing the other dogs in their kennels. "You've got a process. I'll go along and tell you what you need to know."

"What house are you looking at?"

"It's on Cross Street. Belonged to a woman named Mrs. Jones. Her granddaughter's selling it."

"Denise," Karen said as if saying a dirty word. "Figures. She couldn't wait for the old lady to pass so she could cash in."

He kept his features still, but it was tough. *Wow.* "I wouldn't know about that," was the best he could come up with. Karen Bowler pulled no punches.

"Who's your real estate guy?"

"Logan Hughes."

"Good. He's a great guy. You couldn't have better working for you," she said with satisfaction. "But watch out for Denise. She's a snake. We had trouble with her earlier this summer. Helping out a madwoman stalker. Pfft. Stupid woman."

"Whatever that story is, is none of my business. I just like the house." And he'd like to get a dog, so he was carefully noncommittal on the gossip. There was a yellow dog in the end kennel that reminded him of Rex, except for the color. "What about that one at the end?"

"Taken. Going home later today."

"Any others like him?"

"No. That standard poodle would do you if you convince me you're a good candidate."

"A poodle?" He walked over to the kennel and the long-legged, fluffy, black-as-ink dog with a face like a shaggy bear stood on its hind legs. He could reach Max's shoulders if the gate weren't closed. "Taller than I expected." The small, black eyes of a sight hunter gleamed in the shaggy face.

"Tall, lean, and elegant," she said. "Not the frou-frou dogs you assume they are. They're excellent hunters. But they're also clowns and need a lot of exercise." She gave him another assessing glance and somehow, he felt he'd come up short. "On second thought, not for you."

"How about I fill out that application you mentioned, and we start there?" *Rather than telling me I'm a fool for thinking I might be a good dog owner.* "The house I want has a big yard and is down the block from the riverfront park. There's a walking path along the river that goes behind the house."

"It's about a mile long," she said with a nod. "Glad to see you're thinking about the how and where of exercise."

His ringtone sounded and he read the screen. "It's Logan."

She waved at him to go ahead, but he noticed she stayed near enough to overhear his conversation. Fine, whatever, he needed to stay on her good side. Suddenly, having a dog in his life was as important as getting this house.

"Logan, what's the news?"

"The seller is questioning the amount you need to put into repairs. This is awkward, but she wants to walk through the place with you to see what you plan to do. Then she'll decide whether it's a fair offer. She's got stars in her eyes and believes the house is in better shape than it is."

"This is a weird request. But, sure. Can we do it in, say, half an hour?"

"I'll check." He came back to the call a moment later. "That's good, we'll meet you there."

When he explained the interruption, Karen Bowler snorted. "See? I told you she's a snake. Denise will go for the jugular if she can. Don't let her."

"Thanks for the warning." He stepped off to leave and then turned to face her again. "I'll be back."

"You can print the application from our website." She gave him a nod that could have been laced with approval, but he couldn't be sure. "Fill it out and bring it back. We'll see what happens."

Ridiculously pleased he'd passed muster; he patted Beau's broad head and strode away.

KAYLIN WALKED WITH the boys up Cross Street. Three homeowners had offered Brody and Taylor fresh home-baked cookies. But none of them wanted to pay for home repairs, although she pointed out rotten floorboards on their porches and peeling paint on the window shutters. Most of them were seniors and claimed to have family members on the way over to do the work. Still, she handed them her business card and pointed out her website address so they could look at her work for themselves. They were kind, of course, but convinced their family members would come through.

At the end of the third block, she gathered her nerve and held the boys' hands while they crossed the street to begin the return journey. "When we finish our walk, we can go back to the park, but promise not to run away from me."

"Big swings," Brody said. Her stubborn negotiator. He'd only promise not to run off if he got a ride on the swings. Taylor would bolt no matter what he promised not to do.

Two trips to the park in one day seemed like a lot, but the dreary apartment felt suffocating and she stayed out of it for as long as she could. The first thing she'd do when she got some money saved was move into a roomier place. Preferably one with windows she could open. She was convinced the homeowner was breaking the fire safety code by not having windows that worked.

She'd offered to do repairs for him in exchange for a break on the rent, but he'd refused.

Never mind. She'd get work soon and once people saw her results local referrals would pour in. That would go a long way toward her developing a steady income.

When she had a steady income, she could tell Connor to stuff it. And she could pay for a good lawyer to keep his payments coming.

Up ahead, she saw Logan Hughes climb out of his minivan. She'd met with him in his office and he'd seemed impressed with her portfolio of work, but he hadn't offered anything except the name of the developer who was building new homes out by the highway. She planned to take an hour to run out there tomorrow when she left the boys in a daycare in the mall.

Of course, the daycare wouldn't know she was leaving the property, but she had no one to leave the boys with for the short amount of time she'd be gone. She shoved her guilt to the bottom of her worry pile and kept walking.

Logan's passenger door opened, and a stocky brunette climbed out. Logan must be showing the house with the For Sale sign on the lawn. The two-story Victorian had seen better days and Kaylin picked up her pace so she could say a friendly hello. The boys jogged beside her, eager to get to the park. They'd complain about the stop to chat, but she had no choice.

"Hi there," she said with a smile. "Logan Hughes, right? We met the other day?"

"Kaylin Simpson," Logan responded, with a kind smile. The woman looked put out and her gaze raked the boys.

"Are you showing this house?" Kaylin asked.

"I'm selling it," the woman answered for Logan. "You interested?"

"Oh, no, I couldn't afford anything so lovely," she said sweetly. "I do renovations and repairs so if you find anything that needs a bit of polish, I'm your girl." She fished a business card out of her pocket and handed it over.

The woman took it. "I've never heard of you," she said silkily. "Are you licensed?"

"Not yet. I'm a fourth-year electrician's apprentice though and I've also done a lot of carpentry and painting." She'd started out as a house painter for summer work in high school. The pay was better than serving fast food. Over time, she'd picked up a lot of different construction skills.

"If you're not licensed you must be cheaper." The woman's gaze sparked with interest.

As Kaylin considered her comment, another vehicle parked behind Logan's. A man jumped out of the driver's door.

Not just any man.

The man. The one who'd saved Taylor this morning. The non-parent who knew all about raising children and keeping them safe.

"Mr. Whyte," the woman said in a soft, flirtatious tone. "I'm Denise Jones." The woman offered him her hand. "And this is the woman I've interviewed for some of the work you think the house needs. Although, I doubt there's much to do. My grandmother was meticulous in her upkeep."

Chapter Four

Max shook hands with Denise Jones and then looked from Logan to Kaylin and back. Logan shook his head almost imperceptibly. Ms. Jones's claim that her grandmother's house was close to immaculate made him want to choke with laughter, but he controlled the urge. "You forget, Ms. Jones, I've already been through the place. And I'll decide which local firm gets the work."

Then he turned to face Kaylin Simpson and her boys, who stood awestruck at seeing him again. "Hello boys, nice to see you holding your mother's hand like good boys."

Kaylin's pretty brown eyes flared into wide circles of enraged protective motherhood.

He winked but it didn't seem to help. Kaylin's shoulders stiffened at his attempt at humor. Fine. She was touchy about any criticism of her parenting skills, joke or not.

"Let's have another walk through," he said as he rubbed his hands together in anticipation of an exciting round of negotiations with the owner. *AKA a snake who'd go for the jugular.* He cocked an eyebrow at Ms. Jones and at Logan, who'd be playing referee.

He saluted the boys goodbye and motioned Denise Jones ahead of him toward the home's narrow walkway. When he realized that Kaylin and her boys were following close behind, he stopped and turned. "Yes?"

"I'm giving a quote on the work," she said defensively. "Ms. Jones wants me to."

Denise turned from where she stood on the veranda. "That's right. Come right in, won't you?"

He didn't see a clipboard or tablet in Kaylin's hand, but he'd go along rather than lose the first skirmish.

The second the boys stepped inside the house they broke free of their mother's hands and started zooming in circles around the living room, screeching. Apparently, a room without furniture was cause for races and squeals of delight. Logan joined him in laughter at the antics while Ms. Jones's eyes went sharp as razors.

"Keep those brats under control," she snapped at Kaylin, who looked peeved by her boys' behavior and Denise Jones's reaction. "I'm sick to death of children wailing and carrying on. That's all I hear through the school year. Brats."

Kaylin's mouth fell open but before she could reply, Max spoke. "This is what children do, Ms. Jones, and I'd think being employed at the public school, you'd understand. There's nothing wrong with letting off steam. They're excited."

Ms. Jones's eyes widened at his rebuke and Kaylin snapped her mouth shut with a wild glare in his general direction.

Logan wisely moved on to the dining room, testing the floor as he walked. "Got some work in here," he said as he pressed down with his foot. The floorboard bowed under the pressure.

Denise stomped over. "That's nothing."

Max glanced at Kaylin and was shocked to see tears glistening. She sidled over to him and whispered. "I need this work. You've helped me twice today. Can you try for a third time?"

He'd decided not to hire her, but his reasons seemed selfish now. Her adorable twins zoomed around the room, her eyes were wide and desperate, and he'd chosen not to give her a job because he maybe wanted a date.

He felt like a lowlife scum for basing a decision on his romantic aspirations with a woman he didn't know.

"Let's get this over with," he said to Denise and Logan who stood in deep discussion over the floors. As much as he wanted to, he couldn't promise anything to Kaylin until he knew what he'd be doing with the time between now and Christmas. He wanted the house, sure, but he may not get it and sympathy for a would-be contractor shouldn't factor in.

He also needed to learn how hard a negotiator Denise Jones was.

But he soon saw chinks in her armor as they walked the kitchen. She huffed and puffed about every repair needed. It was as if she was seeing the house for the first time. Maybe she'd been sentimental about the place and had seen it through a haze of happy times and memories.

Kaylin followed along, her eyes scanning everywhere at once. She wasn't missing much and from the slight smiles and nods, she already had a vision for the room. Her gaze took in everything, from a stain on the ceiling to the ruined flooring. She appeared decisive and relaxed as they discussed moving the plumbing for a sink in an island and running a water line for a modern refrigerator. She knew her stuff and he felt more confidence in her with each suggestion she offered.

After exhausting the living room and declaring themselves the winners, the boys ran more circles in the dining room. By the time the adults had gone through the kitchen Taylor and Brody were attempting a run at the stairs that bisected the front rooms. Kaylin moved fast and caught them before they'd gone up more than two risers.

"No running on these stairs. Look how high they are," she said firmly with a hand on each boy's shoulder. The stairs were a straight shot to the second floor and a long way to fall from the top.

Max snagged one of them and lifted him to his hip. "Wanna see the basement? It's spooky down there."

Blue-grey eyes as wide as they could go, stared back into his. A thumb went into its customary hole and the boy nodded. Max couldn't be sure if this was the one he'd saved earlier or not. Either way, the kid was interested.

Spooky was cool when you were three.

Denise Jones glared daggers at Logan as if he were to blame for the childish interruption, but Logan was too busy chuckling to notice. Or maybe he did see her expression and didn't care.

Kaylin shot Max a grateful glance while the boy she held onto jumped up and down to go see the spooky room. "Don't assume this counts as the save I asked for," she said in a soft tone.

She needed the work. Judging from the frayed edges of the boys' blue jeans, Kaylin shopped at thrift stores for hand-me-downs. Her own clothes looked a size too large for her. Her jeans hung at her hips and her loose T-shirt sagged around the V-neck. It had been washed a few too many times. Was she losing weight from stress or did she dress like this to hide her figure?

Logan had said her portfolio looked great and that she'd come to Welcome because she'd spent summers here. She was sort of local, but new, too. Being unknown would make it harder in a small town to get a business off the ground.

Kaylin Simpson had two kids and needed the work and Max shouldn't think about her body. If he hired her, she'd be an employee and he knew his boundaries and adhered to them. He let the vague dream of dating her drift away.

Meanwhile, every necessary repair was being denied by the owner.

"Enough," Max broke in when Denise whined about how the banister on the basement stairs was firmly in place. He invited the boy in his arms to give it a shove.

Denise's lips pinched tightly when the banister moved under the boy's hand.

"If a three-year-old can rock this thing, it's dangerous. Look, if you don't want to sell the house, admit it," he said to Denise. He watched her stubborn denial fade away.

The homeowner's eyes turned assessing as greed filled her gaze. If he looked closely he'd probably see her nose twitch like a rat's. He wondered what Karen Bowler would say about the look on Denise Jones's face.

This was going better than he'd hoped.

"I want to sell," Denise muttered, barely audible. Max smiled amiably at Logan and Kaylin.

"Then, let's talk money and a closing date."

"The sooner the better for me," Denise said. "I want out of this town."

LABOR DAY

Kaylin sat in Candace Markham's living room with her hands folded in her lap. "I got a contract to renovate a house. Can we barter daycare for my boys now?"

The daycare operator was a single mother, like Kaylin, and her home needed work. Kaylin held her breath because while they'd talked about bartering on a couple of occasions, the other woman hadn't agreed yet. If Kaylin couldn't find daycare for barter, she couldn't work. If she couldn't work, she'd have no way to keep Taylor and Brody. Connor would never take them, not even for a short time. And she couldn't ask Aunt June and Uncle Mack for help. They were fine, but there wasn't a lot of extra money.

She hoped her desperation didn't show, but Candace was looking back at her with deep sympathy in her gaze. Candace smiled easily and Kaylin felt a small relief.

"You're in luck," she said. "One of my clients has decided to move suddenly and take her two children out of state." She waved her hand. "Family stuff, she said, but I didn't ask."

"Oh, I moved quickly, too. So..." Kaylin trailed off.

"Normally, you understand, I'd have my spots filled. There's room right now if you grab it. But I'll expect a lot of work completed if you want to keep them here."

"We'll work it out," Kaylin assured her, feeling shaky with relief. She'd run out of daycare options weeks ago as her savings had dwindled. "I have two weeks before work begins on the house on Cross Street. I can start here immediately. I appreciate that you've lost the income from those two children, so I'll work fast. And I'll be able to pay you from my first paycheck."

Candace brightened. "That's great. The sooner the better."

"Let's look at your priorities. I'll start there." Brody and Taylor had already invaded the play area as if they belonged, so the two women took a seat within view of the children and started a list. When they finished, Kaylin looked at her list to see what each job entailed. There was nothing here she couldn't do. "Would you mind if I took before and after photos to add to my website?"

"I'll do better than that," Candace said. "I'll add them to my social media pages and the Welcome online group. People will know your name by Christmas."

Christmas. Maybe she and the boys would have a real Christmas after all. "That's wonderful, I'll give you a list of things I'll need so I can begin right away." She made notes on her phone about what parts she'd require for the first job and shared it with Candace. "I'll measure the sink so you'll get the right size."

The other woman read the list on her phone and grinned. "I'm tired of that leaky faucet. With the dripping my water bill gets higher all the time. And a new sink will look great."

Kaylin pulled up a website on her phone. "Here's a faucet and sink that will work. The new sink will sparkle and new stainless is easy to clean."

The other woman's expression glowed. "I'm excited. And how boring am I if a new sink gives me the warm and tinglies?"

Kaylin laughed. Candace, with her bright green eyes and sunny expression, made Kaylin feel hopeful and she hadn't felt that way in far too long.

"Want to stay for hot dogs? I've got a nice salad ready, too," Candace offered.

"Really? That would be awesome." She did a quick calculation, and this free meal would stretch the money that Connor had sent her for another day. "I can't reciprocate for a while though. Money's tight."

"I get it. Why else would you be bartering?" Candace stood, clearly not expecting an answer. "Hey boys, are you hungry?"

"Yes," Brody and Taylor chorused.

"Good, because I have hot dogs with your names on them," she announced. "I hope you like them grilled."

"Yay!"

Kaylin wanted to cheer, too. They wouldn't have to return to the apartment she'd now started to think of as a dungeon. Not for another couple of hours, at least.

Half an hour later, Kaylin helped set the picnic table outside in Candace's roomy backyard. "This table could use a sanding and some new paint."

"Yes, it does," Candace said ruefully. "But there's only so much time in a day."

"I could throw it into our bargain."

Candace shook her head, her dark curls bobbing. "No. I couldn't do that; it wouldn't be fair. With fall coming soon, we won't be using it much. I can take care of it next spring."

"Okay." Kaylin set the last plate on the table and began laying out cutlery. "But the offer stands." Candace's daughter, Dayna, was five and wanted to help. Kaylin supervised as the girl carefully lined up the forks beside each plate.

Candace turned the hot dogs on the grill and then opened some buns to set on the top rack. "Tell me more about the job you got," she said, sounding interested.

Kaylin warmed. "I'll be working on Denise Jones's grandmother's house. The man who bought it hired me today." It had taken another day to negotiate, but in the end, Denise accepted that she wouldn't get a better offer. And apparently, she was in a hurry to get out of Welcome.

The buyer, and the twins' personal hero, Max Whyte, had turned out to be an okay guy. He'd explained how scared he'd been when he saw Taylor run into the road. He'd even apologized for taking his fright out on her when she'd walked up to thank him. *Awkward.* "The new owner is Max Whyte and he's new here, too. I was basically there at the right time."

"Lucky break," Candace said with a nod. "You mentioned it was on Cross Street. I know the house. Fixing that place up will take a while. That old woman was so difficult with people that even if she did want to hire help to fix things up, they'd have charged her extra. Nasty. I don't like to speak ill of the dead, but that woman..." she trailed off and tsked. "She enjoyed stirring up trouble. At least, that's what my parents used to say, and they remember her well."

"The house has been neglected for years. It's rough. Max wants me to get lots done before Christmas, so I'll need a helper. Max will be hands-on but he works in Redmond so the bulk of my time will be spent without him in the day." He'd mentioned he could install drywall and wanted to do the basement walls on weekends. Fine with her. She'd see how good a taper and sander he was. Lots of men exaggerated their handyman skills.

"Please remember," Candace said, waving the barbecue tongs around, "to pick up the boys on time."

"I will." It felt good to chat with another woman her age, with some of the same concerns. Candace had a child to raise and ran a successful business out of her home.

Kaylin wanted to be in the same position sometime soon. Independent and solvent. A home and backyard would be a bonus if she could make it happen.

"I'm sure you'll try and that's all I ask." Candace sighed tiredly. "I have long days and some parents assume a few minutes here and there don't matter. They squeeze in after work errands and it's not fair."

Kaylin felt for her. Depending on people to be on time could be a problem. "If your parents knew Denise Jones's grandmother, did you know Denise?"

"Oh, sure. I heard she's leaving her job and heading to Italy with the money from the house sale."

"Is that so? That sounds exciting." And different.

"Oh, there's another thing you should know about the house on Cross Street." She leaned close and raised her eyebrows. "My mom says the place is haunted."

"It's pretty old so I'm not surprised there's a haunted story. I'm sure several people have passed away in the house over the decades. But plenty of babies would have been born, too. So that evens things out." She laughed. "Haunted or not, if I inherited that kind of money, I'd buy a house right away and save the traveling for when the boys are older."

"If it weren't for help from my parents, I'd be renting, so I hear you." Candace put the wieners in the buns on a plate and whistled for the children. "Come and eat you three."

After they ate their hot dogs and creamy coleslaw and salad, Kaylin offered help cleaning up. "You know what? I'd appreciate a hand," Candace replied. "The kids are fine outside and I'm enjoying talking to an adult. I don't have a lot of company."

"Me, too, about the adult time," Kaylin said with a heartfelt sigh. "I can't remember having people over for dinner." Connor didn't count. "At least, not since I had the boys."

"All the more reason we should make our arrangement work. Aside from my house being repaired and you getting daycare, we need grown up company." She offered her hand for a high five and, with a grin, Kaylin slapped her palm in agreement.

After cleaning up, they sat at the kitchen table with a pot of tea between them and half an ear on the children who played happily together. "Your daughter has attitude. I like that. My boys can be overwhelming."

"Pfft, my Dayna can give orders like a general. Mostly, she gets away with it, but sometimes the other kids rebel and then I have a heck of a time restoring order. I'm glad she's off to school tomorrow. She needs the structure and to learn to listen to an adult leading a class. It's hard for her here with the other kids with me being her mom."

"Moms and daughters," Kaylin said vaguely, remembering her loss with a pang. Three years and she still thought of her mother every day. "Are your parents still living?"

Candace nodded with a fond smile. "My mom owns the Welcome Bakery. She's from Jamaica." She fluffed her dark curls. "Dad went on a grad trip and came home married."

"Nice. And they're still together?"

"Of course. Dad says he invested eight months of his life in convincing her and he's still waiting for the investment to pay off. Accountant humor."

"You're lucky to still have them." Kaylin had seen the bakery, but couldn't afford to go in. Not yet.

"Mom's a rock and my dad is great, too. He gave me my green eyes if you're wondering. His family's Irish."

"I wasn't wondering," she said. "They're beautiful." She sipped her water. "If I had a built-in family business, I'd be ecstatic, but you don't work in the bakery."

"I had to when I was younger, but my mom and I butted heads too much." Candace laughed softly. "Plus, I hate to bake. Cooking? Sure. But pies are harder than they look." She waved her hand in a swirling pattern. "Pastry has to have the right hand, as my mom explained continually. I didn't know what hand she was talking about, so I quit trying and it became painfully clear I wasn't destined to be a baker." She chuckled as if at a memory.

"And your father's an accountant?"

"Yes, he's the one who convinced me to run my daycare and invest in this house."

"He doesn't do repairs for you?"

"No. Not handy in the least which my mother teases him about whenever she can."

"You had a happy and whole family." Some people did. Kaylin wanted badly to give that kind of family to her boys.

"I did. It's fine that my dad can't fix things around here. They're both busy with their businesses and it's up to me to figure things out on my own, or else what's the point? It's my house and my business."

The firm set to Candace's chin meant Kaylin had found a kindred spirit. "What will your father say about our barter?" Without numbers and arithmetic would it make sense to him?

Candace grinned. "We've struck a good bargain we can both live with." She eyed Kaylin. "What about your parents? They don't live around here?"

The inevitable question.

"No, they don't. I had an aunt and uncle here who were like second parents. I stayed with them for summers when I was a kid." She smothered the ache in her heart with determination. "My parents divorced, and dad had a new family in no time. Mom passed before my boys were born. She knew they were coming, but never got to see them." The tears had dried up long ago, washed away by her other worries.

"And their father? What about him?"

"If he was there for us, I wouldn't have to barter."

"Enough said. As for me, I learned some men lie about everything." Candace sighed. "Except for my dad and my brother, of course."

"Of course," Kaylin said in stout agreement as she wondered what lies Max would tell her.

Chapter Five

Max stretched out on his bed and settled in for a video chat with Willow and Lily. They'd been in school for four days now and the upcoming weekend with them would be full. After the usual small talk and exclamations about their new schools, he got to the point. "I'm filling out an application to adopt a dog from a local rescue." He held up the sheet of paper so they could see for themselves.

Both girls squealed. "What kind? A puppy?"

"When will you get it? Will it be a girl or a boy?" Willow asked.

"I'm not sure about anything except I'd like a Labrador or golden retriever or maybe a shepherd." An image of the shaggy poodle crossed his mind's eye. Too frou-frou. Besides, Karen Bowler had said she'd changed her mind about him being a good fit for the poodle. He frowned. "I'll see what breed will work best with our situation. Whatever dog we get it'll need walks twice a day." He planned for a morning and evening walk along the river walkway.

"What about a tiny dog like the celebrities have?" Lily asked with an excited shiver.

"Something bigger, Lily. I don't want a bitty little pup that would look like a snack to a hawk or eagle."

"Eww! Dad! That's gross," Lily cried.

"Besides," Willow chimed in, "this isn't Vancouver Island. There aren't as many eagles here."

"Hawks though," he said, laughing at Lily's disgusted expression. Farmland meant hawks and the area around Welcome was farm and horse country.

After that, the conversation turned toward the house and his move to Welcome. He'd be glad to get out of the hotel in Redmond and get his things out of storage.

"I've hired a woman to do a lot of the renovation work," he said, thinking they'd consider it cool that he thought outside the box when it came to traditionally male roles in the workplace.

Karyn said he should open their minds to different careers and Kaylin was a prime example of outside the box. So far, Willow hadn't mentioned a burning desire to be anything but a mom when she grew up. "Maybe you'd like to do a job shadow with her sometime, Willow."

Willow looked surprised, but halfway interested, so he considered it a win.

"Why did you hire her?" Lily asked. "Is she pretty, is that why?"

He had a lot of work to do with his younger girl on the outside-the-box stuff. He'd enlist Karyn's help with it. Her husband Cade had three daughters and oversaw a big custom home building operation, so he had reasons to get in on this, too.

But Lily the matchmaker waited for her answer. "No, I didn't hire Kaylin because she's pretty. I've seen her portfolio and have talked to her references. They like her and say she does a good job."

"So, she's not pretty?" Willow asked.

He felt hot under his T-shirt collar. "I guess. I don't know," he blustered. "I hired her because of her experience and price. She's new in town and wants to get more local referrals so I got a good deal."

"What's her name? Kaylin what?" Lily asked. Willow disappeared from the screen.

"It's Kaylin Simpson, why?"

Lily shrugged and looked to the right where her sister had gone.

"What are you two up to?" he asked. Because they were always up to something.

Ten long seconds later, Willow leaned back in and held her phone screen up to their shared laptop. "See? She is pretty. Maybe you didn't notice."

Willow's phone showed a picture of Kaylin from her website. A professional photo taken in a studio didn't do her sunny smile justice. In the picture she had her lips closed and her eyes looked serious.

"Stop now. She also has twin boys about three and I'm sure a very full life. I didn't hire her for any reason but her ability to get your rooms and my kitchen ready before Christmas." And because of the frayed edges on the boys' jeans.

"She's married?" Lily looked crestfallen.

"I don't believe so. I got the impression she's a single mom." He spoke without thinking, because his mind jumped to the desperate way she'd asked for the work.

His girls exchanged smug glances at the news, and he wanted to smoosh their faces with a wet facecloth to wipe their smirks away. After a couple more leading comments he finally got them off the topic of Kaylin. He could never let them meet her.

They'd see what he saw immediately. Kaylin was sunshine and fire and nothing like her professional staged image on her website. So much for his job shadow idea for Willow.

Those twin boys were strong reasons to ignore Kaylin's wide smile, soft-looking mop of curls, and her sparkling eyes. He expected they'd have their disagreements with these renovations but instead of dreading an uphill battle, Max looked forward to sparring with her. She'd looked surprised when he'd mentioned that he'd drywall the basement, but he'd have the last laugh there. He was an excellent drywaller with a steady hand for taping and mudding.

TAYLOR AND BRODY SLEPT in Kaylin's double bed in the bedroom while she slept on the sofa. They needed the room and she'd developed a new sleep position where she'd honed the art of hanging her feet sideways off the sofa. The weird angle had almost become comfortable.

Until she moved.

Or woke up.

Or needed to stretch. Like right now.

Her alarm went off and she rolled to the floor. Propping herself up with both hands, she rose to her feet. Seconds later, she wrinkled her nose against the mildew smell in the bathroom. No matter how many times she scrubbed it, the tiny room stank. Having no tub meant the boys had grown accustomed to showers but she hated that they couldn't play with their bathtub toys.

She used the rickety toilet, glared at her groggy face in the old mirror and then wondered how soon she could ask for an advance on her pay when the job with Max hadn't even started.

Her thoughts moved on to finding a helper she could afford. Candace might be a good source. She made a mental note to ask her.

She finger combed her hair and remembered she had to get her clothes out of the landlord's dryer before he came downstairs to check. He didn't like that she insisted on using his machines but, too bad, she couldn't afford to go to a laundromat, and she'd told him that when she'd moved in. She kept her machine use to a minimum by washing delicates in the bathroom sink and hanging them over the shower rod, curtain rods, and kitchen chairs.

The sound of giggles announced that the boys were awake and already playing on the bed.

"I'll be right back," she told them from the doorway. "I'm going to get our clean clothes," she said. "Then I'll get your breakfast."

"Bacon." Taylor said the same thing every morning and every morning she shook her head.

"Not today. Someday soon, though." With her first paycheck, she promised herself. The promises she'd made around that first paycheck began to stack like the boys' old building blocks.

She dressed them and packed their lunches for daycare. Today, she'd be working on Candace's kitchen sink. She'd double checked with Candace last night that she'd got all the parts Kaylin would need for the job.

She scooped her hair up into a ponytail, grabbed an elastic band that had previously held a stalk of celery together and ushered her boys out to her old pickup. She buckled them in and headed to her first real day of work since returning to Welcome. She couldn't wait to start earning money for her labor, but until then, she'd manage with the barter system. Without daycare there'd be no way to work, so today was an important first step.

She liked Candace and hoped this arrangement worked out for both of them. They said to never do business with friends, but this felt right. And Candace most definitely felt like a friend.

EARLY THURSDAY EVENING, Max called Kaylin. "The sale's complete," Max told her. He stretched out on his bed and felt the week at work drift away as he imagined her chocolate eyes warming at the good news. They'd both been waiting for this day to come. "You can start in the morning. I'll meet you there."

"This must be the fastest deal in the history of real estate," Kaylin responded a bit breathlessly. "I'm so glad."

"Logan recommended a lawyer and Denise Jones hounded the guy until he dropped everything else and got things done. She's already booked her flight to Italy."

"My friend, Candace, told me Denise told the principal of the school to stuff her job up her butt and cackled like a crow on the way out the door. Talk about burning bridges."

"You've already got a source for intel in this town?" He chuckled. The only people he knew in Welcome he could count on two fingers and he was talking to one of them now.

"The Welcome Bakery is where it's at if you want to learn anything about anyone. I haven't been in there yet, but Candace's mom is the owner."

"And who's Candace?"

"My daycare provider. I'm doing some work for her in exchange for daycare so I can get paid to work for you."

"I see. You're resourceful." If she were married, he thought, she wouldn't need to barter for childcare. He wouldn't let his girls know; it was bad enough that he'd already let it slip that he thought she was single. No need to confirm.

"I don't know about me being resourceful," she responded slowly. She hesitated as if she wasn't sure how to take his compliment. "I'm desperate."

He heard a smile in her voice as she admitted her situation. He hoped it wasn't dire, but the humorous tone made him wonder if she was making light of her struggles.

"Good to know about the bakery," he said to move past the awkward moment. "I'll check it out someday." He'd enjoy some fresh baked pastries now and again and the girls had their favorites, too. "Hughes Realty is right above the bakery. Smells great up in his office."

"Yes, it does. And that reminds me," she said. "I'll need a helper. Could Logan recommend a laborer? He knows most people in town. He might have a line on someone dependable who's looking for work. Candace didn't have anyone in mind."

"Since I'll be at the office while you're working at the house, you will need another pair of hands." And likely a bit of brawn now and again. "Asking Logan is a good bet." He'd hate for her to have an accident or fall when she was alone on the job. "I'll call him now."

"No, thanks, I'll do it. I have specific questions to ask him about a helper if he recommends someone."

"Sure thing." They set a time to meet and he hung up, wondering what kind of guy would be spending long hours in Kaylin's company at the house.

SEPTEMBER 20

The Friday she was to start work at Max's house, Kaylin waited out front for him and Logan. Logan was stopping by with a spare key for her that he'd gotten from Denise and Max wanted to confirm the plans he had for the kitchen.

Hmm. Max's ideas were good, but he expected a lot if he wanted the kitchen completed by Christmas. New plumbing, wiring, and a higher amp service took time and the first day of fall was tomorrow. The holidays were coming up fast.

While she knew how to do the wiring, the new electrical box would need to be installed by a qualified electrician, and then inspected by a building inspector before it could pass code. She gritted her teeth that she'd walked away from her apprenticeship, but she'd had no choice. Somehow, she'd find a way to get her license, but that was a worry for another day.

She leaned against her truck fender and crossed her arms over her waist while she waited. The first to arrive was Logan. She waved and gave him a smile he returned as he climbed out of his family-friendly van. SUVs were more popular, but his minivan could haul a houseful of kids and all their stuff.

After they greeted each other, Logan tossed her the house key and followed her up the walkway to the front door. The key stuck, but with another turn, the door opened with a creak.

"Sounds spooky," she muttered. "I've heard this house is haunted."

"I don't believe that," he said, "unless you count mean-spirited people."

She looked at him, surprised by the comment. "Actually, I do mean them. They can leave a bad taste." Candace had told her that the Joneses had hated her parents on sight. Denise had been nasty to Candace and her brother, too.

"Before Max gets here, I want to thank you for giving my brother a chance. Jamie will work hard." Logan had explained his younger brother had had a battle with painkillers. He'd been clean for most of a year. But it was an uphill battle for him to get a job when the good folks of Welcome knew his story. He had support from his family, but not a lot from the other people in town.

"Max hired me and gave me a chance. Least I can do is pay it forward."

Logan grinned and put his hands on his hips. He looked at the ceiling in the dining room with an experienced eye. "Between you and Max, giving people breaks, the good vibes will blow the leftover bad ones right out of here."

"I hope so," she said.

"This is tin plate on the ceiling. Will Max keep it?" Logan asked.

"I hope so. It adds charm. We can fish wire through to re-wire the light fixture. But that's easy."

"Great to hear you say that," Max said happily from behind her. She spun to face him. "Because I want to keep the ceiling as is."

Her employer stood with his face raised to the ceiling, his throat strong and straight. With his two top shirt buttons open she got an intriguing peek at his chest hair. His hands were at his waist and as his face lowered to the room, he grinned and caught her gaze. Her breath caught. She'd just seen Logan in this exact stance but hadn't noticed a thing.

"I don't know about you," Max said, "but I'm excited by what we'll do with this place."

Logan slapped his hands together. "It's great to see the before and after." He told Max immediately about their plan to have Jamie work with Kaylin.

And the end of the explanation, Max had his arms folded across his chest and a frown on his face. He stared hard at Logan. "You say your brother's dependable, but I don't want Kaylin faced with delays because he doesn't show up the day after payday."

Max had a point, even as blunt as he'd been. This was serious business. Addicts with money made for lost days and nights. She swung her gaze to Logan's.

The handsome real estate broker firmed his lips and nodded. "Jamie's doing great. He's strong, but I hear you. If he slips up, let him go and I'll help you find someone else. I'll keep my eyes open, too. If I see any familiar risky behavior, I'll have a word with him." He scrubbed his hand down his face. "But I believe he'll do fine. He wants to. His life derailed for a while, but he has a future. Not so long ago we didn't believe he did."

Kaylin got hung up on the "let him go" part. It would be up to her to give Logan's brother the news that he was fired. Was she prepared to do that? She'd never been in charge before. But admitting her nerves over firing someone seemed unprofessional.

Besides, it may not come to that, so she kept her concern to herself.

Max studied her face and nodded. "If he needs firing, I'll do it."

Chapter Six

Kaylin looked put out by Max saying he'd fire Jamie Hughes if needed, but these were not regular circumstances where he hired a contractor and crew. The contractor was responsible for his crew in that case. But with Kaylin not having a crew of her own, men she trusted, he had to step in if required. She was his employee and if she needed back up from him, she'd get it, whether she wanted it or not.

"Let's not hire Jamie with the idea of firing him before he even shows up," Kaylin responded tartly. "Logan says he's feeling strong and committed to staying clean. He deserves the benefit of the doubt."

Max hoped for their sakes that this worked out.

A flash of gratitude crossed Logan's features and Max nodded his agreement. "Okay. If Kaylin's willing to see how this goes, then I'm in." But he'd keep an eye on things between Jamie and Kaylin.

"Great. I'll call him when we're done here," Logan said. "He'll be happy to hear he's in."

"Wait, he does have experience with hand tools, right?" she asked. "I should have asked before, but I assumed that he would since you recommended him."

Logan nodded. "Our father kept us busy in his workshop. And Jamie's strong and fit. These days he works out to help in recovery."

"Fair enough." Max's response covered both him and Kaylin and she nodded in agreement.

"I'll leave you to it, then," Logan said and after shaking hands with both of them, headed toward the front door.

When they were alone, Max and Kaylin looked at each other.

"Why are you doing this?" she asked. "Giving me a chance? Letting me give Jamie a chance?"

He shrugged because he wasn't sure of the answer. But she needed to hear something, so he said, "Everyone needs a break at some point, and this is your time. And I won't lie and say seeing you with those boys on your own didn't affect me. Having you ask for the job the way you did stayed with me."

"So, it's pity?" Her eyes narrowed as if she didn't believe it.

"Not completely." He grinned to allay her fears. "The fact is, I like smart women. Women who're determined to succeed. My ex was one of those women and I admired her for it. She opened a Christmas store, of all things, and made a go of it."

She pursed her lips as she considered his comments. "And?"

"I liked what I saw online about you. I especially liked your expression when we saw the kitchen during our walk through with Denise Jones. You had a vision for the room, and I wondered what it could be. But I couldn't ask in front of Denise." He wouldn't tell her that her previous employer felt responsible for her sudden exit from her job with him. There was a story there, but Max wouldn't press her for it.

She nodded and seemed satisfied with his answer as far as it went. A mischievous smile lit her face. "Let's go compare notes on what we'd like to do in there."

Was she flirting? No, of course not. He steered his thoughts away from her unintentional double entendre.

"Lead the way," he said and waved for her to go ahead of him.

The kitchen would best be described as a farm kitchen, but since this house had been built in town, he suspected it harkened back to someone's childhood and they'd replicated the farmhouse kitchen. "This room is huge and there's still a walk-in pantry with another sink and an exit to the side of the house. They probably delivered goods there."

"A service entrance," she said. "Do you want a mudroom in that space? A two-piece? There's already water there for the sink. It would be easy enough to plumb for a bathroom."

"A mudroom, yes. Board and batten for the walls. And hooks and shelves for coats and boots. A two-piece washroom on the side. I'd like to keep the extra sink. Make it deep. Big enough to bathe a big dog."

"Why not put in a full bath? A big dog will need more than a sink." She cocked her head. "I didn't realize you had a dog."

"Not yet. But I want one. The girls say they want a tiny one, but I'd like a larger breed."

"Girls?"

"Yes, my daughters, Willow and Lily."

"A dog and daughters," she repeated, looking surprised by his answer. Maybe he didn't seem like a dad to her. Not in the way Logan did with his family-toting van.

"A wife, too?" she blurted, with flashes of red high on her cheeks that intrigued him.

"No wife," he said. "I have an ex, though. She's remarried. But we're friends. We were better at being friends anyway, so we're good." He leaned against the kitchen counter and crossed his ankles and his arms, settling in. "So, why come back to a town where you don't know anyone to help you get your business off the ground?"

She scuffed the linoleum with the tip of her steel-toed work boot. "I always liked Welcome and I needed a new start. From scratch," she replied.

"And you have no family here?"

"No. But, I'm doing okay." She smiled lightly as if she hadn't a care in the world. "Look how fast I got work with you. And I'll have a helper soon and my boys are in a good daycare."

"You had to beg for this job." Too late, he saw how that sounded. "I didn't mean..."

She shrugged off the awkwardness of his comment. "I'm not stupid enough to be proud. Yes, I need this job, no question. But you'll get value for your money. This project could make a big difference for me. This street is full of houses that need the kind of work I'll be doing here. Also, I'm bartering daycare for repairs, too. Candace tells me she'll post about me and my work on a town page." She made a face. "I may be living broke, but I have options."

"Seems to me you've found those options on your own." Another reason Max felt good about working with her. Kaylin was resourceful and determined to make a life in Welcome. "You're to be admired."

"As to that bit about homes on the street needing the same kind of work. When we're finished, I'd like to invite the people who live nearby to stop in to see what I've done."

"Like a showcase for your work?"

"Exactly. That is, if you don't mind. I'll bring cookies and coffee. You won't have to do a thing, I promise."

"Except keep out of your way for a couple of hours?" He wouldn't though. He'd be here, talking to the neighbors and supporting Kaylin.

She laughed and nodded. "I'm using up valuable daycare hours with this chit-chat. Maybe we should move on," she said and tapped notes into her phone. She waved it at him. "Full bath and mudroom. Next?"

"I want the kitchen and my girls' bedrooms done before Christmas. Take notes on the kitchen. The island goes here with a sink on this side." He pulled up a drawing on his tablet. "I'll share this with you." He liked the idea of a farm sink with a high curved faucet with a sprayer attachment.

"Got it. Could you print it, too? I don't have a printer."

"Sure. We can keep a copy here for Jamie if you're not around."

"Good. There's nothing you want to keep in here?" Her gaze swept the decrepit fixtures and walls.

"Take it apart. I want the board and batten in here, too. We might as well follow through from the mudroom."

"Agreed. But the board and batten goes on the bottom half only. That'll leave the top half smooth so you can paint or wallpaper if you choose to accent."

"And that's why I hired you. I could tell you had a vision."

She flushed and he quickly moved away toward the hall so he couldn't get caught up in looking at her. "Now, I'll show you which bedrooms I want done first," he said brusquely.

She followed him, friendly chit-chat behind them. He'd taken her measure and she'd taken his.

Except he wasn't certain that she was single. Not that it mattered. He didn't want to know anything personal about her. He knew enough.

On the way upstairs, he said, "If Jamie has an issue around taking orders from a woman, tell me."

"If he has an issue like that, I'll fire him myself."

"Good."

Chapter Seven

"What do you know about Kaylin?" Lily asked Max from her side of the screen. This girl, right here, should be a lawyer, arguing cases in court. She'd be killer at cross-examination.

"Lily leave it alone. Kaylin works for me." The video chat had taken another beeline into his love life and he wasn't sure how. But his youngest was a dog with a bone about Kaylin. "I don't need to know anything personal about her. Also, there are rules that shouldn't be broken around employee/employer relationships."

Was twelve old enough to be told about sexual harassment? And worse? Inside, he groaned. How much had his wife talked to them about the crappy behavior of some men? Give some guys a bit of power and they couldn't wait to throw their weight around. He frowned at his dark thoughts.

Willow elbowed her younger sister. "Yeah, haven't you heard of the movement calling out gross old men who prey on young, pretty women?" His elder girl rolled her eyes at her sister, but Max wanted to hear Lily's answer.

Max sighed. "Willow, there's more to it than gross men and young women, and I'm sure not every older man is disrespectful." Hell, *he* was older. Staring at forty. Did that make him a gross old man? In his teenage daughter's eyes, probably. Likely in Lily's eyes, too.

A lot of men his age had much younger women. Second wives often brought second families. But that wasn't for him. Max wasn't interested in teaching a woman who Green Day was or what life was like before cell phones had cameras.

If he had to guess, he'd put Kaylin in her early thirties. Not young, exactly, but younger than he wanted in his life. Not that he wanted her in that way.

Yeah, tell yourself another lie.

Any man with eyes would want her that way. He hoped she wasn't single because that would be tempting. And if she were, he hoped it was temporary; like her husband was in hospital or the military and would be home soon.

Then he had a scary thought. What if she was running from a husband? Hiding from a man who'd hurt her?

Or hurt her kids?

If that were the reason for her returning to Welcome; a town that didn't remember her, he sure as hell wouldn't want a man to show up looking for her.

Nah. That wasn't the reason she'd needed to start new from scratch. She'd never have a website with contact information on it if she were in hiding.

"Dad? The screen's not frozen, but you're not moving or talking." Lily had her head tilted like a curious cat. He blinked.

"Oh? Sorry, girls, but I've got to go." He needed to talk to adults, not to his kids. They got into his head and the conversation around Kaylin wasn't a good idea.

They said goodnight and he headed downstairs to the hotel bar. The bartender was a good guy and they'd shared a couple of laughs.

After he enjoyed a cold beer, he called Logan Hughes.

"Hey, Logan, got a minute?" He tapped his credit card on the bar. He kept his personal expenses separate from his living allowance because he didn't want an accounting department keeping track of his occasional after-hours beer. And shooting the breeze with a bartender wasn't a business expense.

Logan yawned in Max's ear. "Sorry about that," he said with a chuckle. "The twins are finally asleep, both sets, so yeah, I've got a minute."

Max heard paper shuffle in the background. Logan was busy so he'd make this quick. "It's time I made some connections in Welcome. Is there a decent place to meet up with people?"

"You mean women?"

"Yes," he replied. He wouldn't be averse to meeting a nice single woman. Maybe that would push Kaylin out of his head. He huffed out a breath. "But I'm wondering about people I might have stuff in common with. I spent my life in Nanaimo aside from university and, well..." he trailed off, aware of how pathetic this sounded.

"You're looking for guys to hang with?"

"I guess. Maybe a running buddy? Or a touch football team for old guys?" He should have searched online, but he hadn't thought of this until now. When the bartender had mentioned a beer league at the bowling alley, the comment had given Max a nudge to look for something social to do.

"Come running with me and Clay Foster," Logan said. "He's the veterinarian. I don't get to go as often as I used to, so he'd be happy to buddy up. Saturday morning?"

"Great. I'll be there. I'm camping out in the house on Friday night anyway."

JAMIE HUGHES HAD TURNED out to be personable, hardworking, and an all-around nice guy, Kaylin thought. He took direction well and wanted to be part of a team. Turns out, he'd played football in college so the team playing came naturally. On Friday, to say Kaylin was relieved was an understatement. She'd been telling Max all week how pleased she was with Jamie's work.

The kitchen had been ripped out in no time and he'd helped her muscle the old cabinetry and torn up linoleum into the trash bin in the driveway. He didn't pester her with too many questions and worked efficiently.

If Jamie hadn't been sidelined into addiction, he'd have made a major success of his life by now. They hadn't talked about his situation, but you'd never know by casual conversation that he'd had a problem with painkillers.

They sat side by side on the front porch steps waiting for Max to appear. "I hope he gets here soon because I'm due to pick up my boys." She checked the time on her phone. Thirty minutes, plenty of time if Max got here soon.

"You said they go to Candace Markham? I remember her from Welcome High. How is she doing?"

"Good. Her daughter has started school and I was lucky to get my boys into her daycare."

Jamie's raised eyebrows reminded Kaylin that he'd been out of the loop regarding his school friends. Addiction stole so much more than the obvious. "I never heard she'd had a daughter."

"She does."

"A husband?"

"Nope."

Jamie looked away, down the street, as if it didn't matter in the least what Candace was up to these days. Kaylin wouldn't offer any more information on her. They'd become friendly and it wasn't up to Kaylin to gossip. She'd tell Candace that Jamie had asked after her though. No harm there.

"I can cut up that fallen tree over the weekend if you want. My parents could use the firewood," Jamie said.

"It's okay with me unless Max has other plans for it. I didn't include that in the estimate, though."

Max pulled up and parked. He waved as he climbed out and walked to the back of his SUV. He opened the hatch and then pulled out a sleeping bag and cooler.

"I guess he's staying here," she said to Jamie. Max seemed happy and excited as he gathered his gear.

"Looks like it." Jamie nodded to Max as they rose to their feet to greet him. They'd met a couple of days before when Max had come to check on their progress. "I was wondering if you want the firewood from that tree in the backyard?" he asked Max.

"If you need it, take it," Max responded. "I'm going with gas for the fireplaces." He set his gear on the ground and headed back for more. He pulled out a thick stack of books and his laptop.

Surprised, Kaylin was curious about the titles, but she couldn't get a good look at his preferred reading material.

"I can carry those," she offered. He passed them to her. She looked at the stack. "Nothing fun in here," she quipped. They were books about real psycho killers and true crime.

"They help me sleep," he said with sly grin. "I like knowing they were caught."

"Thanks for the firewood," Jamie said to Max. "Logan and I can cut it and load it up over the weekend."

She wondered briefly if that was Jamie's real plan for the firewood. Selling it was an easy way to get cash his family wouldn't know about. Addicts could be sneaky. But, if Logan came to help, she'd know Jamie was well-intentioned.

Jamie picked up his empty lunch cooler and walked to the sidewalk. "I'll be going. See you tomorrow. I'll bring my dad's chainsaw." He strolled off in the direction of the park, like he did every evening. She could only assume he walked anywhere he needed to go.

Kaylin helped Max take his gear into the house. "Want the books where you'll be sleeping?"

"Yes. I'll keep my things in the same room. I don't want to interfere with the work." He led the way upstairs and turned toward the front bedroom. "This room's mine," he said as he shouldered his way past the door into the room. "Eventually, I'll want to take the room next to it for an ensuite bath and walk-in closet."

She set the stack of books on the floor by the closet door. She'd already seen the girls' rooms, but not this one.

"I suspect the room next to this was a nursery," Max said. "It's small and under the wallpaper, I found a sunny yellow paint. There looks to be a toy box built into an alcove with drawers and a couple of clothes racks above it. Compact and practical."

Kaylin wandered into the room he'd described. "I've been focused on the work on the main floor, so I haven't seen this room." She took it in with one turn of her head. "Yes, a nursery at one time."

He was right to turn this room into a closet and bath. She imagined walking into this room and sinking into a tubful of bubbles. She'd have candles on the windowsill over a sleek freestanding tub with a high back and room to stretch out in. Heaven, she thought.

She chuckled to herself.

"What's so funny?" Max said from right behind her. She hadn't felt his presence at her shoulder because she'd been lost in her reverie.

"I was daydreaming about a tubful of bubbles and then the twins raced in and wrecked the whole fantasy."

He grinned. "Yeah, I get that. My girls at their age never gave us any privacy."

"Even when I ask them to leave me be, they insist on opening the bathroom door." She cringed inside at the earthiness of her sharing a snippet of her family life. But kids...

"Tell me what kind of tub you see? And the other fixtures," Max said, in a practical tone, as if she hadn't just admitted she peed with the bathroom door open half the time. "How would you lay out this room?"

He stepped around her and stood with his arms crossed, surveying the space. But there was a tension in his shoulders she hadn't seen before.

With Max, she pretty much noticed everything.

He swung his handsome face toward her. He had sexy fine lines at his eyes and a sprinkle of whiskers that softened his jaw. His eyelids drooped as he swept his gaze down to her toes. "What would you like in this room?"

She wanted to gulp with the sudden heat, but that would be gauche and young and too revealing. "You don't pay me to fantasize, but I'd want a freestanding tub with the faucet on the side so two people could share."

His eyes flared with interest, and she wanted to take back the words, but they were out there now.

"Or a mom and a set of twins?" His joke broke the tension, and a wash of gratitude rolled over her for the humor.

"Fat chance I'll get time for a soak in a bubble bath anytime soon." She pointed to the far wall. "Twin pedestal sinks over there with drawers between them and a counter on either side."

"The shower?" He arched an eyebrow. "On the left?"

"Yes. But big with lots of heads."

"Of course."

Dear heaven, he was killing her just with his eyes, so focused and intent.

Chapter Eight

Max had flirted. With her! Half of her said she shouldn't be stupid, that he'd never look at a woman with her kind of baggage. But the other half, the half that still believed in happiness and contentment, that other half said, "Why not me? I'm in good shape, have a nice personality, don't kick dogs, and I'm resourceful, like he said."

That half? Should shut the heck up. There was no room in her already-too-busy life for flirting.

Especially not with her boss. The man who signed her paychecks. The man who held sway over her life.

"For now," said that traitorous half that should mind its own business.

Kaylin cleared her throat and moved out of the room and out to the hall. She pretended interest in the railing while she gathered her thoughts.

Soon, she'd be able to pick and choose her jobs. She had to have faith that Max would recommend her to people who asked. Also, there was the work she was doing for Candace. She cocked an eyebrow at Max. "Candace has already posted about the improvements I've done at her place."

"Great," he said. "I'm sure people will notice."

But would that be enough to land her real work doing bigger reno jobs? A flicker of fear wormed along her insides. What if she did something Max didn't like, or she didn't respond to his smiles and jokes? He could sabotage her and her fledgling business.

The last time she'd ended up at odds with her boss, she'd hauled herself and her sons halfway across the state to get away. Had to start over. Had to live hand to mouth.

She would not let that happen again.

Max looked over the railing to the staircase. "The railing is far sturdier than what we found in the basement, so you can stop trying to tear it apart."

She smoothed her hands down her thighs. "Oh, right."

She looked at him. "Look, I came to Welcome to have a life. A *good* life. To raise happy, healthy children here. To have a career and business I can be proud of. I'd like to pass it along to Taylor and Brody if they want it."

"Yeah," he said. "That's what most business owners want."

"Yes. I'm no different." The men she'd worked for had wanted to build businesses, too. And they weren't shy about asking for what they wanted. "I'll need your support. Recommendations and stuff like that." She raised her chin.

"You'll have my full support," he promised.

"Good," she said with an air of having made a pact.

Maybe, she'd find someone to love who loved her back. But it couldn't be Max Whyte. Not now.

Shaken by her thoughts, she followed him downstairs. His mind had turned inward, and she was fine with that. She didn't need sexy smiles or charming quips to fend off.

She collected her backpack and aluminum water bottle, signalling the end of her work week. She had fifteen minutes to get to Candace's for her boys. Plenty of time.

"Jamie seemed eager for the firewood," Max commented. "He worked out okay?"

She'd told him on the phone throughout the week, but he still wanted confirmation. "Yes, the tear down of the kitchen would've gone slower without him. I'd still be hauling cabinets to the trash bin if not for him."

"He didn't try anything?" His gaze held hers.

"What do you mean?"

He frowned and turned toward the door so she couldn't see his face. "You're young, pretty, and he's a normal guy alone with you all week. You'd tell me if he was bothering you."

"He's not bothering me and, believe me, I've seen the signs." The only interest Jamie had shown in a woman was simple curiosity about Candace and there was no harm in that.

"It's my responsibility to provide a safe work environment and I take that seriously. If anyone steps out of line, tell me." Max rooted around in his backpack and brought out a rectangular binder. Business checks. "And if you know the signs that means you've had some experience with harassment." He cocked an eyebrow at her.

She nodded. "I'm a woman doing what people think of as a man's job. I know when a man is interested, and I know how to say no." She looked levelly at him, without flinching. She felt good about not flinching.

One error in judgment had taught her a lot. Two errors if she counted staying with Connor for far too long. She frowned. Her judgment with men needed an overhaul.

Kaylin stepped back a pace and studied Max as he wrote a check, signed it, and tore it out of the book. "Give me an invoice for this amount and we'll go weekly from here on in." It wasn't the usual arrangement, but she was grateful.

She flushed hot and took the check, slowly. She didn't want to appear anxious. "Thanks." She looked at the amount. It was more than enough to cover her time and Jamie's hours. "I'll pay Jamie out of this. When he shows up to get the firewood, let me know and I'll stop by."

"Good." He nodded. "I'll call you tomorrow. If you have time, I'd appreciate your input at the supplier's, too."

She frowned. "I'll have the boys with me. No daycare on Saturday."

"No problem." He turned away. Over his shoulder, he said, "They can come along. My ex tells me my choices in my last house were too masculine." He chuckled as he walked through the dining room. "I should've taken her with me when I was ordering material. I've learned my lesson."

She followed him to the front door. Max seemed friendly with his ex, but he'd said as much. They'd lapsed into the friend zone during their marriage and it had fizzled out.

"So that's why you want my suggestions? Because I'm a woman?"

"Sure. Also, you've done a lot of reno work and seen a lot of mistakes. If you've got good ideas, I'd be a fool not to ask your opinion."

"And you're not a fool," she added with a grin. "Okay. If you can tolerate the twins, I'm okay with volunteering for a Saturday morning."

"I'll pay you for your time. And for lunch. I'm sure the boys would like some chicken fingers and fries?"

"Their favorite," she quipped as she folded the check neatly and slipped it into her jeans pocket. And she wasn't foolish enough to refuse a free meal. And the boys would like to see Max again.

For some reason, Taylor and Brody had taken to him. Might have been the spooky basement and how natural he was picking them up and talking with them. He had a knack with kids despite her first impression of him as a know-it-all non-parent. "See you tomorrow."

He walked with her to the front steps. "We're going to build something good here, Kaylin."

"Yes, Max, we are." She stepped down the steps to the walkway. "And I'm thirty-four. Not so young," she said, as she walked away without looking back for his reaction.

SEEING HER TOMORROW with her kids? Stupid move. Max watched Kaylin climb into her truck and head down Cross Street. He'd seen relief in her eyes when he'd passed her the check. They'd first agreed on payment bi-weekly, but she was hurting for money and he couldn't see making her wait another week. Not with those boys depending on her.

He had an inkling she'd be spending her Friday night buying groceries. The idea reminded him that he needed to pick up supplies if he was camping out in the house. He opened the hatch of his SUV and got out his coffee maker and a large empty cooler. Tomorrow he'd go to his storage unit and drag out his grill. He'd buy a new propane tank when he was at the supply store tomorrow.

With Kaylin and her boys. He couldn't remember their names, but he felt sure she'd be calling out to them plenty when they saw those long aisles of tools, drywall, and the other odds and ends of house construction. Then their names came to him. Taylor and Brody.

He'd help keep them away from sharp things. Healthy, active boys were curious, and he'd already witnessed firsthand what could happen when Kaylin was distracted by one and the other took off.

He set up his coffeemaker in the upstairs bathroom, so he had a ready supply of water until his kitchen plumbing was restored. But he had no coffee, or breakfast food. He'd brought in a cooler, but it was empty.

He made a list of food he needed and then headed out to the backyard to check on the fallen tree. Jamie and Logan should have no problem cutting the limbs and trunk for firewood.

The fence across the backyard caught his eye. It was practically falling down. He decided to check with his neighbors on each side about replacing their sections of the fence, too. That way, his whole backyard would have new fencing.

In the morning he and Kaylin would make quick decisions for his fixtures and cabinetry and he'd have lots of time to check out fencing options. No problem.

KAYLIN HAD TAYLOR AND Brody installed in the grocery store cart at Good Value Foods. They'd promised that they would not throw anything to the floor. Mostly, they were good about it except when she picked out a vegetable they didn't like. Taylor hated broccoli and Brody loved it, so she made sure to ask Brody to hold it.

Taylor liked carrots so he was good to hold those.

Good Value Foods was Welcome's discount food store, so she had to pay attention to the best before dates. She owed Candace for that handy tip. The loaf of bread she held was too close to its expiration date, so she shelved it again and dug deeper toward the back of the rack.

"Hi!" Taylor liked talking to strangers and as she stretched an extra inch, Kaylin was not surprised that a man said hello back.

"Got one," she said on a hushed breath. "This one's as fresh as can be," she told the boys, holding her treasure high.

"Hello, boys. Helping your mom?" The voice sent a warm slide of honey down her back. She looked over her shoulder and right into Max's smiling face.

"Oh, you caught me digging through the bread rack." She crinkled her stack of coupons into her hand. He didn't need to know she needed each and every one of them.

"You've got a mountain of food here," he said with a wave over her cart. "Are you about done?"

She scanned the grocery cart and did a quick evaluation. There was enough for a few days of make-ahead meals she could freeze. "Yes, I think so." Thanks to him paying her early.

He had a hand basket that looked full, too. He raised it to waist level. "I came here to fill my cooler and get a few other supplies for the house."

A box of laundry detergent sat in the crook of his arm. "I guess you can't wait to move in," she said when she spied it.

"I'm tired of the hotel. I keep thinking that if I had an accident the report would read that I lived at 'no fixed address.'"

"That would feel strange," she said. She'd come close to homelessness herself. A rush of gratitude made her smile.

"Mom, let's go," Taylor whined, but Brody punched his arm.

"We should go through the same cash desk," Max suggested. "I'll go first, then I'll take this stuff to my car. I'll come back to help you get your groceries to your truck." He waggled his eyebrows at the boys.

"Yay!" This came from Brody whose hero worship for Max knew no bounds. No surprise there. Max had saved Taylor's life. Even at three, Brody understood that what Max had done was special.

She frowned and it was on the tip of her tongue to refuse Max's help, but his light expression stopped her. What harm could it do to let him help? It was a kindness, and the boys needed lunch. "Thanks, the sooner I get these two hungry mouths fed, the better."

MAX HAD KAYLIN'S ADDRESS and out of curiosity, he drove past the ramshackle home that had a room-to-rent sign in the living room window. On the right side of the basement an old wooden door sat with a sign that said Unit B, which is what she'd given him when he'd hired her. If she lived downstairs, then it must be a dark and dreary place.

His lips turned down at the thought of those active, sunny boys living in quarters below street level. He'd bet the place was moldy, too.

Damn it, poverty took a toll. He knew it, logically, but his mind raged that Kaylin and the boys were forced to live this way.

The items in her grocery cart had been bargain brand and save for hamburger and ground chicken, there was little in the way of protein. She'd loaded up on fruits and vegetables that looked more than ripe. Kaylin must have gone through the discount bin with a sharp eye. She'd used a handful of coupons, too.

Max cruised past the house and then turned toward his place. Maybe he'd taken a chance hiring a virtual unknown who was new to town, but he was glad he had. She'd asked him to recommend her to others and he'd be happy to. She'd got a lot accomplished in one week with only one helper.

He bought a propane tank for his portable grill and headed home. He'd picked up a couple of steaks at a nice butcher shop and was looking forward to one. Maybe someday, he'd be grilling two. When he pictured the person he'd be cooking for, Kaylin's smiling face filled his vision.

Damn. Cooking for Kaylin would not be smart.

Not smart at all.

Kaylin was too vulnerable for him. No matter how he looked at it, it would be wrong to pursue her. She depended on him and his paychecks to house and feed her children. Asking her out would be akin to sexual harassment. Kaylin would feel pressured and nothing good could come of making a woman feel like she had no choice.

Hands off, Whyte. She doesn't need any pressure from you...she has enough already.

He felt better for having decided. Kaylin Simpson was safe from him. Completely. They had a professional relationship, her kids were cute, and he enjoyed their happy faces.

But that was all.

Tomorrow, at the supply store, she'd give him her thoughts on the fixtures for his kitchen and bathrooms and that was it. She'd leave him at the store while he checked out the fencing. Yes, that would be the smartest move.

When his house was finished, she'd move on to other work and she and her boys would become a happy memory. They'd see each other in passing and he'd wish her well.

Chapter Nine

"Thanks for coming with me," Max said as he, Kaylin, Brody, and Taylor walked into the big box home building store. The boys were making *vroom vroom* noises and looked ready to take off. "Stay close boys, people are pushing those big flat deck carts around and they could hit you if you're running around corners."

"What's a dickert?"

"A flat deck cart," he said more clearly and with a grin. "Like that one." He pointed one out that was loaded with sheets of drywall. Both boys looked impressed.

Kaylin smiled her thanks. "They've never been in one of these stores." She seamed her lips. "This might take a while. They'll ask a lot of questions."

"Their father never takes them to a hardware store?"

She shook her head. "There haven't been many men to ask questions of." She flushed an interesting shade of pink. "And I've only ever been in these stores during work hours."

"Okay," he said easily. "I brought the measurements of the kitchen." He caught one of the boys gently by the back of his collar. "Don't bolt," he said around a chuckle as he released his light hold. "I *just* explained why you shouldn't run in here."

"Hold my hands," she instructed the boys and reached for them. With a firm grip, she led the way down the aisle toward the kitchen fixtures.

Max followed, relieved she hadn't minded him stopping the boy from running off. He didn't want to overstep, but he didn't want any injuries either.

"We'll take you to the park as soon as we leave," Max promised Taylor and Brody forty-five minutes later. "But we need to look at one more thing." They'd decided on the color for the kitchen cabinetry, but he'd come back to the store with the measurements and order when he was alone. The twins had broken their concentration too many times to trust they'd get the order correct.

"You've said it now. We have to follow through with a trip to the park," Kaylin said through her teeth.

"No problem. The bathroom faucets are over here," he said as he hoisted Taylor onto his shoulders. Brody had already had a ride. He'd given up on the idea of looking at fencing ten minutes after they'd arrived.

SEEING BRODY AND NOW Taylor on Max's broad, strong shoulders gave Kaylin a start. First, she'd been afraid Brody wouldn't hold on. Then she feared her son was too heavy.

But now, she realized with a pang that the boys had never been manhandled in this way. Had never had the fun of seeing the world from up so high. They were enthralled.

And so was she.

After the initial shock, her heart settled back into her chest and she was able to walk without gawking like a girl at Max with her boy on his shoulders.

Since they were only ordering for the main floor mudroom/laundry/bathroom, the fixtures were an easy decision because they were standard. The spa bathroom in the master suite would need more thought when the time came. But she had plenty of ideas on what she'd like. "You'll ask me about the ensuite bath again when the time comes?"

"Definitely," he promised. "Especially now that I've had your input today. You've got a good eye for décor."

Warmth rose in her cheeks and she focused on the boys while she digested his compliment.

"I'll go order and pay, then load your truck first," he said, oblivious to the moment. "I'll meet you at the park with lunch."

"I can run through a drive-through on the way," she offered while making some quick calculations on her bank balance. Maybe she'd spoken too soon. The boys needed shoes and warm coats for the winter.

Max frowned. "I promised to pay for your lunches because you've given me your morning and that's what I'll do. What would you like?"

The boys hopped up and down and squealed out their orders for chicken and fries, while she opted for a large chicken salad. "Thanks, we'll see you at the park." She considered stopping at the Welcome Bakery for dessert but decided against it.

This was not a date. Sharing lunch in the park was payment for her time on her day off. But the boys were excited to spend more time with Max and if she were honest, so was she.

MAX WASN'T SURE WHY he'd offered a take-out picnic in the park, but that's where he, Kaylin, Taylor, and Brody were thirty minutes later. From a grease-scented bag, he pulled out chicken strips and fries for the boys. A container of chocolate milk for each boy followed and the boys' eyes lit up. Hungry, growly sounds filled the fresh air around the table.

Kaylin reached into the second bag and brought out her salad and Max's monster burger and fries. The boys were already busy blowing bubbles in their milk through paper straws.

"Milk is for drinking," their mom said, "not playing with." But there was a smile in her voice that the boys heard because they giggled and shoved each other as they perched on the bench seat.

"I'm pleased with the color choices we made for the cabinets. Co-ordinating them with what I want for the kitchen was a good idea." He'd taken photos and made notes. The order for the custom kitchen cabinets would be easy when he went back to the store alone.

"Sorry the boys were so distracting," she said, wiping dipping sauce off the boys' chins.

"No problem. I need to look at fencing anyway, so I'll order everything I need at once."

Halfway through their meal, Taylor pointed at his mother's face. "You messy dis time."

Kaylin had a smear of salad dressing at the corner of her mouth. She dabbed at the wrong side and the boys giggled and jeered that their mommy was a mess.

Max wrapped the end of his napkin over his fingertip and lightly touched the corner of Kaylin's mouth. Her gaze met his and he zeroed in on her luscious, kissable lips. Her focus softened and her mouth rose at the corners.

The noise from the boys disappeared. A soft sigh escaped her lips.

Her throat moved slowly as she swallowed. Her eyelids fell shut. Her lips parted and with her face turned to his, he'd swear she issued an invitation to kiss her.

He pulled back. "All done," he said and bent to the task of balling up trash and stuffing it into the paper bag. "Thanks for coming with me this morning," he said. "We'll unload our trucks at the house. Yours first so you can continue with your day."

Her gaze turned confused, as if waking from a dream. She blinked and the confusion cleared. Her phone buzzed into the awkward silence. She glanced at the screen.

"I've got to take this," she said with an apologetic glance. "It's my aunt." She took the call.

Only seconds later, it was clear Kaylin had an emergency. Her shoulders stiffened and her voice went high. "Will he be all right?" And then, "Okay, let me know, please. I'll keep my phone on and with me all the time."

She disconnected and set the phone squarely and with great care onto the picnic table. The boys chattered between themselves while she turned stricken eyes to Max's. "Heart attack," she mouthed with a significant glance at Brody and his twin.

Max nodded. As much as he wanted to ask for more details, there wouldn't be many more. She'd only been on the phone for a moment or two. He assumed it was her uncle that was in hospital.

They made a pretense of eating and encouraged the boys to finish quickly so they could talk in peace. The moment the boys were done, Max told them to have fun on the play equipment and watched as they bolted for the playground.

"Do you need anything?" He asked.

She shook her head. "Only time to wrap my head around this. My uncle's such a fitness buff, it's hard to believe. He works out, my aunt makes sure he eats right. He hikes and rides a bike." Her tone was dull with worry.

"Sometimes it's genetic and staying fit delays the inevitable, but heart problems can happen to anyone." He patted her shoulder awkwardly, unsure of what she needed from him. But whatever it was, he'd give it. Her eyes were still filled with shock and fear.

Kaylin nodded. "She'll call as soon as he's out of surgery. They're doing everything they can, she said."

"Do you need to be there?"

She bowed her head. "No. I can't go." But it was clear she wanted to. Her desire to be with her aunt sat heavily in her eyes, in the way she moved like a robot as she gathered the remnants of their paper and boxes and walked stiffly to toss the trash in the container by the walkway.

For Kaylin, the sun had gone out of the day while Max still had a day full of decisions and work to do. As much as he'd like to hang out to be sure she was okay, it wasn't his place to offer that kind of comfort. And no one, no matter how much they wanted to, could be in two places at once.

When she dumped the trash, Kaylin turned and looked at him, lost and alone. She had no one else. Max was it for the moment. He walked to her as she stood by the trash bin.

"I'll watch the boys until you're up to it. It'll be a long day for you."

"Thanks." The word was small and fearful.

"Try not to worry. All his good habits will help him recover. That's why we take care of our health, so when push comes to shove, we have a leg up." Next time he had take-out it would be a salad, not a monster burger.

The boys were headed from the slide to the big kid swings and he loped across the park to supervise while Kaylin took the time she needed to gather her thoughts and her composure. He caught glimpses of her on the phone as she paced back and forth in serious conversation with someone. Was she asking for help or looking for answers from her aunt?

When she came to the swings, her face was stony.

"More bad news?" He asked.

"There are some people you should never ask for help," she responded. "They'll always let you down. Can we unload the cabinets now? I have more calls to make and I don't want to hang you up this afternoon."

He wanted to say it was no problem to keep the boys, but she was determined to handle this on her own.

Back at the house he saw Logan's minivan. The brothers were here for the firewood, so he enlisted their help to empty his SUV and Kaylin's pickup so she could go on her way.

The fallen tree had been stripped of limbs and the trunk was being cut into short logs. With the removal of the limbs the damage to the lawn became clear. He'd need to put down new sod to cover the scars left behind.

It bothered Max that Kaylin had no help during this family emergency. He shouldn't get involved in her personal life, but he'd been there when she'd got the call about her uncle and that was hard to ignore. He'd be stone-cold not to feel sympathy for her.

He cleared the emotions with the reminder that she wouldn't appreciate pity and that something would work out so she could go where she was needed. She'd made it plain she had more calls to make and she was nothing if not resourceful.

He surveyed the yard. With the pile of limbs set to one side and the short logs being removed, the space looked bigger. He turned and gazed at the back of his house. He imagined a new deck off the kitchen and a gazebo halfway down the lawn. Maybe he'd hire a landscape designer to come up with something more imaginative.

Logan stepped up beside him. "You can make this place into a beautiful home."

Max nodded half-heartedly, aware of the possibility of Kaylin's loss. "A home is made up of family. My girls are only with me part of the time." He didn't want to fall into the poor me, I'm alone, place he'd been before, but this house was too big for a single guy.

"You've got them and that's the main thing."

"I'm thinking about Christmas."

"Already?"

"Yeah, I'm pretty sure my girls will want to be with their mother and their new sisters this year." It stood to reason he'd be an afterthought.

Logan looked surprised. "But getting the house ready for Christmas was the goal."

"It still is, but I'm not sure if this place will ever feel like a home. Not to Lily and Willow." Maybe he should see the house as a flip property and not dream about the place being a real home. If he kept this renovation about making money, he would stop griping about being alone in this too-big family home.

"Divorce and remarriage have long-term unforeseen consequences. But your girls are used to moving between houses to be with you and their mom."

He frowned. "I guess."

"Have you asked them about Christmas?"

"No. My father says if you can't handle the answer, don't ask the question."

Logan rubbed a hand down his face. "My wife had a lot of family stuff to deal with when she returned to Welcome. Her eldest son's father had died and suddenly Daniel's grandparents wanted to be in his life. Elle handled it well and now Susan Murdoch is part of their lives and she has us living at her place while we're renovating. We've become this big, weird, loving clan that I never in my life expected to be part of. But I am. We are."

Max eyed him. "So, more family, not less?"

Logan nodded. "Exactly. And let's not forget that Elle's second ex left her for a pregnant young woman and now their twins have their father's new wife and a baby sister in their lives."

Max conceded defeat. "Okay, that's some story."

Logan laughed. "Yes, it was a hard return to Welcome. She had a feisty rep to overcome. That first year for Elle was insane. Meanwhile, I'm falling in love with her and insisting that I want a kid of my own because Jamie and I are adopted, and I thought I had to have my own flesh and blood."

Max shook his head, disbelieving. "You pushed her for *more* children? And survived?"

Logan frowned and looked into the middle distance. "I lost her. I lost my Elle. She left me because I couldn't see a way out of my stubborn view of the world."

"What happened?"

"I had a talk with my father and after that, I understood better about being a dad and how, even when they aren't your flesh and blood, they can still be *yours*. I was coming around to Elle's way of thinking when, out of the blue, Elle showed up at my house and everything fell into place. We got married, had our own twins, and life got less complicated because we communicated. We have a family calendar we live by. Where the kids are for which weekend and which parent and on and on." By now, Logan was laughing. "It's hectic but we're in it together, so what the heck. It's a fine balance, but once the adults set aside their differences and put the kids first, things smoothed out."

Boggled, Max stared at Logan. "And I'm worrying about a couple of days at Christmas." And feeling sorry for himself. And feeling old. And alone. "I'm getting a dog," he muttered.

Chapter Ten

Two days after his picnic in the park with Kaylin and the boys, Max was still pondering his conversation with Logan. In particular, how Logan and Elle had expanded their family to include her exes and grandparents and other siblings.

Some people had an inexhaustible supply of love. He set the idea aside. But his mind couldn't shake how much fun he'd had with Taylor and Brody at the home hardware store and at the park. And then Kaylin got the call from her aunt and her world had tilted.

He hadn't spoken with Kaylin since Saturday, but he'd have heard if she'd been able to find a way to get to Arizona for a few days.

He ran over the morning he'd spent with Kaylin, Brody, and Taylor. This time he allowed himself to think about how much he'd enjoyed talking with their mother; his attractive employee, the woman who depended on his pay checks to feed those wonderful kids. The woman who couldn't be there for her family when she was needed most.

Aside from the bad-news phone call, nothing special had happened. Nothing special at all.

They'd eaten their take-out food at a picnic table while he and Kaylin took turns wiping sauce off the boys' chins.

And then, Kaylin had a bit of her salad dressing smeared near the corner of her mouth. Big mistake to help her with that, but he'd dreamed of her inviting expression both nights since.

ON MONDAY MORNING, Kaylin still had no options for taking a quick trip to Arizona to help her aunt through this rocky, frightening time. Connor refused to take the boys, saying he didn't want to confuse them. More likely, his girlfriend didn't want to have her hands full with another woman's busy three-year-olds.

Candace felt terrible about being away this coming weekend, but she had long standing plans for a family getaway and couldn't take Taylor and Brody.

Kaylin was certain she could get an advance on her pay so she could afford a plane ticket, but she couldn't take the twins with her. Taylor and Brody would be too much for her aunt to handle on top of the worry for her husband.

As much as she wanted desperately to be there, Kaylin had to accept that her only option would be supportive phone calls. Not enough, but that was all she had to give.

Her phone rang and when she saw the caller ID, she put a happier tone into her voice. "Hi," she said. "This is an early call. Is there a problem?"

"Not for me," Max said, his voice a rolling wave of sexy. "And it isn't a problem. I'd like to offer to keep the boys for you if you need to leave suddenly. I can take a day or two off work if needed."

The offer stunned her. Their own father didn't want Taylor and Brody and her boss offers? "I don't know what to say." She felt overcome with gratitude. She blinked back tears.

"How's your uncle this morning?" His question brought her out of her shock.

"He did well with surgery. Three stents are in place, and they expect a full recovery." But her aunt had sounded stressed and still fearful.

"So, it's good news."

"Yes, a big relief."

"The offer still stands if you need some time away."

"Thank you," she said, "I'll keep that in mind." Kaylin was floored by his suggestion. It may be the only way she had to go help her aunt. "Maybe when he gets out of the hospital I could go and help Aunt June get him settled and comfortable."

"If you went next weekend my girls would be here, and they could help with the boys. I'm sure they'd love it."

A spurt of relief brought the sting of tears. She cleared her throat. "I don't know what to say," she repeated. "But be careful because this sounds like a perfect solution. Uncle Mack should be home by then and I could go and cook some meals to freeze and clean the house and make sure they're both okay." One tear from each eye rolled down her cheeks. "I'll install grab bars and whatever else he'll need."

"You go and do whatever you need to do." His voice was so kind, so understanding, she wanted to catch it in a bottle to save for another time she needed cheering up. "I'll see you tomorrow after work," he said, breaking into her sappy gratitude. "I'll leave early to catch up with you then. I have plans for the backyard I want to discuss."

Max had made his offer and then taken the conversation away from the personal and back to professional. She'd be sure to handle herself in the same way when she saw him after work tomorrow.

As soon as her heart stopped fluttering over his unexpected kindness.

ON FRIDAY, AS SCHEDULED, her uncle went home from the hospital. At the house on Cross Street, Kaylin and the twins waited for Max to come home early from work. "Be good for Max, boys. His daughters will be here after supper and they have some fun things planned for you to do together."

Max had told her Lily and Willow were excited to have the boys at the house for a couple of nights. She'd spent the morning boy-proofing the house as much as she could. She'd put hand tools up on high shelves and locked the door to the unfinished bathroom in the mud room so no little hands could get cut, maimed, or smashed by a brother with a hammer.

Taylor clutched his blankie to his chest and Brody held his stuffed tiger by its right ear. The left had been torn off a couple of months back. She smiled and crouched. "How many sleeps will you be here?"

Taylor piped up first. "Two," he announced.

Brody held up five fingers on his right hand. She gently folded all but two.

Brody giggled. "I know how," he said. "This many!" And he held up two fingers on his left hand.

Max strolled into the kitchen, carrying a box that contained a new air mattress. "This is for me. The boys will be on my bed. Will that work?"

She grinned. "Perfect. They share my bed and I'm on the sofa at home."

His brows knit into a slight frown. "You don't have a bedroom to yourself?"

"Not now, but I'm on the lookout for an affordable two-bedroom apartment. If you hear of one let me know. My friend, Candace, is asking around, too, so I'm hopeful."

He nodded and greeted the boys. "Are you ready to see where you'll be sleeping after we have pizza and the girls help get you ready for bed?"

"I don't wanna go to bed."

"Me, neither!"

"I don't mean right now," Max backtracked with a laugh under his words. He began explaining who his girls were amid a new barrage of questions.

Kaylin grinned and sidled out of the room toward the front door. Once there, she picked up her overnight bag and purse, ready to slip away when the boys weren't watching. She didn't want to make a big deal out of her leaving them. They'd be fine here, and she could video chat with them after she got to her aunt and uncle's home.

Brody caught sight of the bag in her hand and ran to her for a hug. Max and Taylor followed her to the door. After hugging them both, the boys looked happy and unconcerned.

"We're gonna help blow up this whole bed," Taylor announced and turned toward the box. Brody bounded up the stairs without a word to her.

Her cue to slip out. With a brief salute, she said her thank you to Max, and gave him a couple of reminders about the boys' routine.

"Their routine is already out the window, by them being here. Go," he coaxed her. "We'll be fine. Lily and Willow will be here in half an hour."

They'd already exchanged the information about where she'd be and her flights, so there was nothing left to say. Kaylin nodded and stepped out into the late afternoon sun. She had barely enough time to get to the airport. Her mind turned toward her aunt and uncle, her only remaining family.

Brody and Taylor would be fine. Staying with Max and his girls would be good for them and Kaylin needed to be with her aunt. Needed to know this heart problem was fixed. Needed to know that in the whole wide world, she still had people who loved her and always had.

Chapter Eleven

O*ctober 8*
Since Kaylin had come home from Arizona a couple of weeks ago, things had been all business between them, and Max liked it that way. He'd wrestled his temptation into the ground, and she'd come home dedicated to the project. Her uncle was on the way to a full recovery and her aunt had promised they'd visit over Christmas.

It was Friday evening and he, Logan, and Clay got to the last one hundred feet of their run and put on some speed. The dash at the end made them laugh as they took turns winning. Today was Clay's turn as the vet bounded ahead on a burst of speed. Logan walked off the sprint, trying to hide a gasp for air. "I need to do this more often," he said between heaves. "I'm falling behind."

"Kids'll do that to you," Clay said. "You've got to make time, or they'll suck it right out of your day." He walked in circles with Max to cool down.

"True," Max said, thinking about the twins and Kaylin, who never got time to herself. "I miss my girls when they're not with me, but they're old enough to leave alone while I run errands."

"Since you're the only single guy here. Got any big plans this weekend?"

"Thanksgiving at my house," Max said. "We celebrate in October."

"You're cooking?" Logan asked.

"I'll try, but it's my first holiday meal."

Clay snorted. "Get help." He shook his head. "How are the renovations coming?" He directed the question to both men.

"We're almost done," Logan said. "We should be in before Thanksgiving. Our *November* Thanksgiving."

"The kitchen cabinets were delivered and I'm still throwing drywall up in the basement. It's slow working on my own, but it's a good workout." That and he was too tired at the end of the night to think about Kaylin. "The mudroom and main floor bath are done. They look great. Kitchen's about finished."

"It's a shame to have that big, beautiful kitchen and cook alone in it."

Clay grinned and took a sip of water from his bottle. "If I had another sister, I'd introduce you, but mine's already taken."

"And the one sister he has isn't a great cook," Logan quipped. "Elle's too busy to do much home cooking." Logan shrugged into a fleece vest as they walked to their cars.

"My sister did a lot of cooking when we were kids. Elle had to or we'd have starved. Mostly out of cans, though," Clay said with a grin.

"I'll find a woman when I'm ready," Max quipped. *And he wasn't ready.* He usually walked home after their run. He liked to mull over his week as he walked.

"Are men ever ready?" Logan asked. "Elle and her kids hit me like a ton of bricks, and I fell like a tree in a mudslide."

"Mercy snuck under my skin before I saw it. I was not prepared for the full-on hit. You probably heard I married her sister, Janna, first."

"No, I hadn't heard." To cover his surprise, he took a slug of water.

"Janna was killed in an accident and when Mercy came home, I was blindsided though I'd known her for years. It's a long story."

"I bet," Max said, patting Clay's shoulder in a man's version of sympathy. "I'm not like you two. I don't want more kids. The girls I have are older. I'm done with little kids," he said, tossing aside an image of Taylor and Brody. "I'd like to find a woman who likes my girls but doesn't want any of her own."

Clay and Logan busted out laughing. "Good luck with that. If I see this mythical woman, I'll let you know."

He waved goodbye to his buddies and walked Main Street to Cross and then to his house, wondering if someday Kaylin would find a man who wanted to be the twins' stepdad. A man Taylor and Brody would look up to and model themselves after. He frowned as dark thoughts crowded him. Whoever the man turned out to be had better be good enough for her. And for her boys.

THE NEXT MORNING IN the kitchen Willow interrupted Max's thoughts. "I love the countertop, Dad," Willow commented and ran her palm across the surface of the onyx top. "It's super pretty. But you look like you hate it." She watched him carefully. "What's wrong?"

Max started and put on a smile. "Nothing, I was thinking about a work problem." Kaylin counted as a work problem, he decided. He palmed the counter, too. "This will look better when it's clean."

"Aw!" Lily groaned and her shoulders slumped. No one could look more put-upon than a twelve-year-old.

"You want us to help clean it?" This, from Willow, who was now scanning the cupboards from top to bottom.

"Reno work is dusty and yes, I need help."

"What about Kaylin? Isn't this her job?" Lily asked.

"Yes, I thought we'd meet her today," Willow said with a sly look at her sister. "We loved her little boys. They're so cute!"

"I've told you before that she has weekends off. She's busy with Taylor and Brody. Besides, the cleaning is my job." He didn't want to hire a cleaning crew when he and his girls could clean. It would be good for them to put in some elbow grease.

"Exactly. It's *your job*." Lily's voice was loud but buried in the exclamation was sly humor. "But I guess we can help."

"There's no guessing about it. I've got everything we'll need right here." He walked into the mudroom and returned with two buckets half-full of warm water and suds. "I'll treat for pizza when we're through."

"We'd have got pizza anyway," Willow commented. But she held out her hand for the bucket.

Halfway through the cleaning, which was going faster than he'd anticipated, there came a knock at the front door. Three taps and then three more in quick succession.

He wiped his hands dry and went to answer. Through the glass of the door, he could tell his visitor was a woman, but that was about all. In October, some people were in hats and gloves.

He opened the door and blinked. "Mrs. Bowler, hello." A dog sat at heel doing its best to stop a wiggle of excitement. "And who is this?"

Mrs. Bowler looked down at the dog. "This is the poodle you saw the first time you came by."

"But he looks different." Nothing like the hairy Teddy Bear Max recalled. He heard a delighted squeal behind him and naturally, the girls crowded his back to get a better look.

"He's so sweet," they sang in tandem, trying to edge by Max to get closer to the dog. He fanned out his arms to hold them back.

"Don't crowd a strange dog," he said. "Wait until you're told he's friendly."

Mrs. Bowler gave the girls the once-over and smiled tightly. "He's been groomed, of course, that's why he looks different. My parents bred prize poodles, so grooming is not a problem for me. What you see here is a sporting cut. Very plain but serviceable for a dog not in shows." She arched an eyebrow in expectation.

"He looks so...regal?" Willow said, clearly wondering if she had the right adjective.

Max agreed. "Yes, regal is the perfect word. Please, come in," he said to Mrs. Bowler. He had a suspicion this was a plot to offload a dog he didn't want, but still, the dog was handsome and lively looking. The poodle's nose was narrow and pointed and Max wondered if there was a reason for shaving off the fur there. Maybe he got into something disgusting.

"I'm surprised you came over," he continued as he stepped back to allow their visitors to enter. He couldn't resist greeting the dog with an ear rub and a good scrub down his lean sides. "Good boy," he crooned. The dog leaned into his hand, begging for more. He wasn't sure he'd ever felt such soft fur.

"I always do an inspection before granting a dog to a prospective owner. Having a dog is a huge responsibility." She eyed the place with avid interest as she entered. "Especially an athletic dog like a poodle."

"Athletic?" He'd seen the dogs before, of course. Most of them looked delicate and had tiny, shaved feet, and pointed faces. Hardly what he'd call athletic.

She smiled widely at him as her gaze roamed the living room and dining room. "You've already made changes here, I see."

The living and dining rooms had barely been touched. He vaguely recalled sweeping them one night because he was sick of stepping on things that crackled underfoot. The mantels had been cleaned, too, rubbed with a wax polish that made the wood glow.

"You've been busy in here," she said with approval. "That woman let her grandmother live in very dusty conditions, in my opinion."

"That woman being Denise Jones?"

"Naturally."

"I'm glad you like the place so far. There's a lot more to do. Mainly upstairs, the basement, and the backyard," he said with a wry grin.

"But let's get back to the dog." His girls had surrounded the poodle and the dog wriggled his whole body. "He seems to love the attention."

Max didn't want to get sidetracked by talking about the house. Not when Mrs. Bowler stood here with a dog and his girls were vibrating with excitement.

But he had questions. "Whenever I've shown up at your kennels, you've found ways to put me off." He'd stopped by weekly since he moved his belongings into the master bedroom. He'd hesitated to invite Karen over while the renovations were underway. He hadn't wanted her to deny him a dog because of a half-finished home.

"There are things I need to explain about this dog," she said, "and I wanted to be sure you're committed."

He'd been committed to a pup, but it looked like that was a non-starter. He'd wanted what he thought of as a man's dog, not a prissy thing. Still, he'd made progress and he didn't want to backslide by insisting on a non-existent pup. He had to work with what was right in front of him.

But Mrs. Bowler was interested in the house, so he said, "We're cleaning the completed kitchen if you'd care to see it. You'll see what we have in mind for the whole house."

This place would be a showpiece and there was plenty of room for a dog. He'd be certain to point out his plans to replace the rickety fence. And he'd remind her of the walking trail beyond the fence.

"I'm amazed at the work you've done," Karen said with a note of awe as she walked into the kitchen. "It's so different from what I remember. I visited when I was a girl."

"Thanks for your warning about Denise. You were right. She was...interesting."

"Yes," she responded drily. "She caused us a lot of trouble last summer and Welcome will be a better place without her."

No wonder the woman had left quickly. She was living under a cloud here. *Not his business.* "I already have a vet lined up," Max said as he walked to the slider to present the view of the backyard. "I've got a jogging buddy with a practice on Main Street."

"Clay Foster is the reason I'm here," Mrs. Bowler said as she took a hard look at the flooring. "How will you feel if the dog scratches these floors?"

"They're non-scratch and I've been assured they can handle a dog. It's a small price to pay to have the companionship."

Willow elbowed Lily. "See? I told you he's lonely."

He cocked a menacing eyebrow at the girls which they ignored. They settled one on each side of the dog. He nuzzled at their necks one at a time as they squealed with delight.

"You wouldn't bring this dog here when my children are with me to torture them," he said firmly. "Clay reassured you?"

"He speaks highly of you," she conceded. Then Karen smiled deeply. "Of course, I wouldn't torture children." She unhooked the dog's leash and opened the slider. "Take him outside to show him his new yard." She turned to him again. "I expect you'll replace that fence?"

"Already ordered the fence panels for the whole yard."

The girls and dog were gone in a bounding ball of youth and energy. Laughing and running and barking, the three companions romped.

"I wanted a pup," he said, but he couldn't help the swell of affection he already felt for the poodle. "I see what you mean about him being athletic. Those leaps and twirls are spectacular."

"I'm glad you like him. I'm fussy about who gets poodles. Not everyone is suitable for the breed. Like a lot of big dogs, he became too much for the other owners and they turned him into the rescue. Poodles need a lot of exercise and grooming every few weeks is costly, but they're a healthy breed." She gave him a steady look. "Your commitment impressed me and the other volunteers. He's only nine months old, so technically still a pup. He'll need more training. I believe he'll be happy here."

Max had stopped by on his days off and had chatted with a few volunteers but only Karen could decide if he'd get a dog. Happy his dedication had paid off, he said, "Let me grab my check book before you change your mind. I'll be right back, and we'll celebrate with coffee." He strode out of the room.

"I'll make the coffee, if you don't mind."

Max slammed to a halt inside the dining room. He turned and grinned through the doorway at her. "Make yourself at home, Mrs. Bowler. You'll always be welcome here."

"Call me Karen," she said with a pleased smile. "I have supplies for the dog in my truck. A starter kit."

"What's his name?"

"It was Jackson, but you can change it if you don't care for it."

"He's used to it now and it's a great name." He took the stairs two at a time so he could grab a check from his makeshift desk in his room and then he could tell the girls they had a pet.

Brody and Taylor would be delighted with Jackson. He couldn't wait to tell them. They'd shared a great weekend when Kaylin was away, and he'd grown fond of the twins. His girls had enjoyed the time with them, too. Happy thoughts danced as he gave up the idea of cleaning the rest of the kitchen. He and his girls had more important work to do.

Namely, introducing Jackson to his new home and walking partners.

"ARE YOU SURE YOU WANT us there?" Kaylin asked Max. He'd called and invited her and the twins to his place to meet their new dog. He sounded so excited. Breathless about it. Brody and Taylor had come home from their sleepover weekend at Max's full of stories and giggles about Lily and Willow, but Kaylin hadn't met them yet. She wasn't sure that she wanted to or that she should.

She'd been content with things being strictly professional with Max.

Mostly. Unless he was doing something like stretching, or lifting heavy objects, or exposing his forearms, or smiling, or making a joke, or carrying one of her boys.

Or breathing.

She sighed and ignored her thoughts, tucking them away under a rock in the basement of her mind.

"It would be best for the boys to meet Jackson when I'm here," Max said. "Do they have experience with big dogs?"

"No." Another thing she hadn't exposed them to, she mentally conceded. Her mom's dog had passed before her mother had and Kaylin hadn't had the time or the money to get a dog, although she loved them. "I love dogs," she admitted. "But I haven't met your daughters. Do you think that's wise?"

It was a broad hint that things were moving out of the professional realm and into the personal. She held her breath as the phone went silent.

After a moment, Max replied. "I figure we're both new to town and we've both got kids who need friends. We do, too. We can be friends, so our kids have each other. It won't be for long because my girls will age out of wanting to entertain young kids, but I don't see how it can hurt any of them. Or us."

"Or us," she repeated, liking the sound of his plan. "Friends, then. We'll be over in half an hour."

She'd had a hard but satisfying work week and she was proud of the work done on Max's kitchen. Hoping his daughters liked the end result, she mentally rearranged her plans for the day. She'd hit the Good Value Foods after they met the dog. Then she'd get fuel for her truck and take a big load of laundry to the Wash 'n' Suds because her landlord had installed a lock on the utility room door.

Fine. At first, she'd been angry about his childish response. But now it was proof she needed to move ASAP. She'd start looking for a new place to live today. By the time she had the boys dressed she was wearing a smile. She hoped her dungeon of an apartment took months to rent after she moved out and her landlord got rotten tenants next time.

She'd wanted to put those moments at the home supply store and in the park with Max out of her mind, but since then when they'd shared a laugh or admired what they'd accomplished together in the kitchen she'd experienced warm and friendly thoughts. *Friendly*.

She needed to focus on being friends with Max so Taylor and Brody could have Lily and Willow in their lives for a while. She'd have a babysitter if they kept in touch and if she started dating, a good sitter would be a necessity.

She also needed a great reference from Max when his project was complete. Candace had spread Kaylin's name around. She'd had to order more business cards because Candace wanted to put them up around town for her.

Slowly, Kaylin was building a support system in Welcome and she couldn't afford to ignore Max's friendly gesture. Plus, she wanted to meet the dog and to see Max.

Of course, Kaylin harboured a tiny crush on Max separate and apart from their work relationship. But her crush would fade by the time the house was finished.

She had some nerves around meeting Lily and Willow. Teen girls could be a whole new level of challenging.

"Boys, if you need the bathroom, please use it before we get into the truck." She wasn't sure why she asked when neither of them ever went without being taken.

"I don't have a pee coming," Taylor said as he studiously clipped one plastic block to another to finish building a tower.

Brody was busy running his car across the sofa back and didn't bother to respond.

"I appreciate you're busy, but you'll be too excited to go when we get to where the new doggie is." They only had accidents when they were too busy having fun to heed nature's call. And playing with a dog would be way more fun than stopping for a pee.

"What new doggie?" Brody asked as his toy car stalled on the downhill toward the sofa arm. His grey-blue eyes went wide. Their pretty eye color was the only thing Connor had given them.

"Max has a new dog, and he wants you to meet it."

"Now?"

"Yay!"

"Is Lily there?" Brody asked.

"And Willow?" Taylor wanted to know.

"Yes, they're there."

Screeching with delight, both boys zipped to the bathroom, crossed their streams, forgot to flush, and then bounced in their sneakers with excitement.

She had them flush the toilet and then wash their hands while she ran a comb through her hair. Lip color would wait until she was parked in front of Max's place. The boys were too wired to wait one more second.

Chapter Twelve

Max watched from the living room window as Kaylin and the boys climbed out of her vehicle. She smoothed her hands down her jeans and suddenly turned away. She rummaged for something in her purse and bent over to peer into the side mirror. The boys ran toward to the door while she slicked something on her lips.

It must be hard to find time for make-up and hair styles with two active boys. They took turns banging on the front door. He knew this because he could hear them claiming turns in loud, excited voices.

"Boys!" Kaylin called as she trotted up the walkway. "Stop yelling, please."

The irony of her yelling about them yelling made Max grin like a fool when he opened the door with a flourish. "Come in, Brody and Taylor. Why are you here?" he asked in mock demand.

"To see a new puppy," they chorused.

Taylor added, "That's what Momma said."

"Yeah, that's what she said." Brody turned toward her and scowled. "Momma, did you fib?"

Ignoring her boys, Kaylin narrowed her eyes at Max. "This better be good. And there better be dog breath and dirty paws involved."

"I wouldn't lie about a new dog. I promise." The promise was made to the boys as he ruffled each head in turn. "If you go outside to the backyard, you'll find Lily and Willow and our new dog playing. His name is Jackson."

Karen Bowler was still in the yard, instructing his daughters on care, exercise, and feeding. She'd know best how to introduce the boys to Jackson.

"You're sure you want me to meet your daughters?" Kaylin asked him as her boys scampered off to meet Jackson. The weekend at his house had made the two twosomes a foursome of buddies. It hadn't taken them long to figure out they could gang up on Max and wheedle more treats or delay bedtime. "Because I could leave them here," she said. She hooked her thumb over her shoulder in a half-hearted gesture. "And hit the grocery store."

"You don't want to meet my dog?" He put on a mock frown.

"I'd love to," she admitted with a smile in her eyes. She stepped inside and he closed the door behind her. "I'm not convinced meeting your daughters is smart."

"It's my weekend with them. They're complaining about it, though because I had them cleaning the kitchen. Then Jackson arrived." He gave her a wry smile and when she looked nervous, he wondered why. "Is there a problem?"

"I never thought I'd meet them." Kaylin chewed her lip and swept a hand over her hips to straighten her jacket and jeans. She wore a purple sweater that brightened her cheeks. "Girls that age are...interesting."

He barked a laugh. "You can say that again. They've studied your website."

Her eyes rounded in surprise. "They haven't."

Max wasn't sure why he was telling her, but he'd come this far. "They wanted to see why I hired you. Now, they tell me it's because you're pretty."

She flushed and backed up a step. "I hope you told them it was my skill."

"All I had to do was show them how this kitchen turned out." He moved toward the slider to look into the yard. "Now, they consider you kickass—their word, not mine—and want to check out how buff you are."

"Buff?"

"I assume they mean your upper body strength." He let his gaze linger on her curious face and laughing eyes. "Your arms and stuff."

"I'll leave that alone."

Now it was his turn to flush. "I think that's best." He offered her coffee. "It's fresh-brewed." After he poured, he said, "The girls said you posted on your website about Candace's praise for the work you've done. Good idea."

She nodded. "Thanks, every bit helps." She looked out the slider and gasped. "Is that Mrs. Bowler?" She blurted in surprise. Their quiet moment dissolved as Kaylin slid open the door and stepped outside.

"You didn't tell me you knew her," she said over her shoulder to Max as she moved across the lawn toward the older woman. "Mrs. Bowler? Do you remember me?"

Max was acutely aware that his daughters stopped their play to stare at Kaylin. Lily went still and quiet, but Willow narrowed her gaze and ran it up and down and then looked directly at him. One side of her mouth quirked up as if to say, "Not bad."

He frowned back. He didn't need his daughters sticking their noses into his business and ruining his good intentions to be nothing more than friendly with *his employee.*

Karen turned at the sound of Kaylin's voice. "Is that little Kaylin?"

"Yes! Yes, it's me. I'm so happy to see you."

Max watched the women joyfully reunite as he stood with his empty coffee mug in his hand. His heart lightened. Kaylin had finally found someone in Welcome who remembered her fondly.

AFTER SEEING MRS. BOWLER out of the blue, meeting Willow and Lily felt surreal for Kaylin. After a major hug from Karen, one of her Aunt June's friends, she soon became surrounded by children. Her boys squealed and demanded a dog of their own. *Of course.*

"We can't have a dog right now," she replied vaguely. Taylor and Brody stamped their feet, but otherwise kept their whines to a minimum. They were learning that most times the answer was no. She refused to feel guilty. Soon, when money wasn't so tight, she'd say yes more often.

Jackson sat nicely beside Karen Bowler. "His fur is silky," she commented while trailing her fingers through Jackson's beautiful, fluffy head and ears. Soft and warm. "He's beautiful. What do you say boys?"

"Yes!!" Taylor and Brody squealed. Jackson's head swivelled toward them. His excited wiggle said he wanted to play some more.

Mrs. Bowler released him and off they went to the back fence to run in circles, leaving her facing two interested female faces. "Hello," Kaylin said, "nice to meet you both."

"I'm Willow and this is Lily." Willow glanced toward Max, but she couldn't tell what Willow was silently signaling to her father. "And poodles have hair, not fur. That's why they need to get it cut so often." She said it smugly, as if she'd known this tidbit forever.

Kaylin nodded. "So, is that why sometimes people dye the color?"

The older girl raised her eyebrows. "It's vegetable dye so it doesn't hurt them." Her voice lost its defiant tone as she glanced at Mrs. Bowler, who nodded along with her.

Lily stared at Kaylin. Hard. "You're prettier than your website picture," she burst out. It was hard to tell if that was a good thing or a bad thing. Lily's expression was noncommittal, and Willow looked appalled at her sister's tactical blunder.

"I had no idea how pretty you both are." Lily was dark-haired and curves were already appearing. Willow was tall and long-limbed, like her father. Both girls were beautiful and cautious with her. Both girls had been sweet and helpful with Taylor and Brody and that counted for a lot. "Your dad says how smart you are and how friendly and kind. It goes without saying that he knows you're gorgeous."

These girls probably scared him, too. As a father, he'd be hyper-aware of the boys who'd flock around them in a couple of years.

They were smart, she decided. Smart enough to see there could be something brewing between Max and Kaylin, even though Kaylin wasn't sure what, exactly, the brew meant. *Could be* didn't mean *actually* and if she and Max kept things on a professionally friendly basis, she'd be happy.

"How does this work; you working with our dad? Do you see him every day?" Lily asked. Willow tried to elbow her sister in the ribs, but Lily dodged the hit.

Kaylin chuckled and Karen Bowler guffawed. "This is fun," Karen said. "I haven't been around tweens and teens in years." To Kaylin, she said, "That's what they call them now, right? Tweens?"

Kaylin flashed her a look that begged her to back off. "I video chat with your dad if I need to show him something in the house. But not every day," she replied with a cool smile. Sometimes, he gets home from work early to walk through the house with me and see what I'm working on next."

"So, you don't go out for dinner to discuss things?" Willow asked in a leading way, hopeful way. Blatant matchmaking.

"Girls, quit with the third degree," Max broke in. "I've told you how things work around here." He looked at Kaylin with an apology in his gaze. "Sorry. They're interested in the reno process."

"Right," Kaylin said with a laugh as the girls looked at each other and competed for best eye roll ever.

"I CAN'T BELIEVE MY luck," Kaylin told Max an hour after being squeezed breathless by Karen Bowler. "To meet up with Mrs. Bowler right now; with the kitchen done and looking so good." After meeting Willow, Lily, and Jackson, she'd talked to Karen about the renovation plans and how she'd come back to live in Welcome. Not the sordid details, of course. Only the upside.

Max sat next to her at the kitchen island as they watched their children play with the dog outside.

"She was full of compliments. But she was more excited when she found out it was you behind the work and the color choices." Max's voice rolled over her, touching her secret parts that she hardly acknowledged anymore. Three years without a man could do that.

She'd quit trying to talk herself out of her reaction to Max last week when he'd made her breath catch as he's stretched up to the ceiling and installed the light fixture. His jeans had eased down a bit and his T-shirt had ridden higher, exposing a lean, firm belly.

She'd forced herself to look away before he caught her gawking. But now she saw nothing wrong with a healthy woman enjoying a nice view.

"Karen is a sweet lady under her bold and assertive demeanor," she explained. "But she's a major source of gossip in Welcome." She checked her watch. "She left fifteen minutes ago so that means most people in town will know I'm here and that I've done this work." Karen had told her she'd talk about her on the town's online gossip group. "She calls her group the 'concerned citizens' of Welcome, but you know what that means."

"Gossip central." He chuckled. Max smelled of expensive aftershave that wafted to her nose when he shifted. Today, he wore a long-sleeved red T-shirt and newer jeans than he usually wore for working.

"You're taking the day off from renos?" she asked with a glance that swept him from head to toe.

He nodded. "I changed when Karen arrived. We were cleaning, but with Jackson here, we'll spend the rest of the afternoon getting to know him. I plan to walk the riverfront path with him and tire him out."

Her gaze slid to the bounding and dancing dog. "He's been running circles around the kids for over an hour. So, good luck with the walk because he hasn't slowed down one bit."

"Karen said she'd leave him here for a day or two and then check back in with us. She seems to think we're not ready for a dog."

"Pfft. That's her way of keeping you on your toes. She wouldn't have come here if she had any doubts about you. Aside from being a gossip, she's an excellent judge of character." That's what her aunt had said about Karen.

"She seems glad you're here."

"I should have known she'd remember me. My aunt and uncle will be happy to catch up with her over Christmas. I'm sorry I didn't look her up immediately. She and her daughter, Brianna. I had no idea Brianna would still live here."

"Apparently, she came home a few months ago to help her mom after a knee surgery."

She reared back from him and widened her eyes mock surprise. "Look at you with all the knowledge. Who's feeding you this information?" She'd assumed he was still alone in Welcome, with no contacts. Silly. He was handsome, friendly, and kind. A great catch for the single women in town. Of course, he'd make connections. Some of them female.

"I have friends in high places," he teased. "Logan, mostly. He and his buddy, Clay. He's the town vet. We run together when we can, and they've filled me in on lots of stuff." Brianna being back in town would certainly be interesting to a single man. As Kaylin recalled, Brianna had been sweet, shy, and smart. Kaylin didn't think those traits would be any different now.

"And they say women gossip. So, you're settling in okay?" She didn't want to ask about Brianna because that would be dangerous. Max might think she cared in more than a professional way.

He nodded. "Yes, I'm making headway. I've got a couple of buddies to have a run and a beer with. My kids like the town and my house. Now, I have a dog for company when the girls aren't here. Life in Welcome is good."

"You'll have a happy Christmas with all you have going on."

"It's only a few weeks away and I'm looking forward to it more than I expected to. New traditions and all that. Until I saw this kitchen, I was considering being out of town for Christmas. Leaving the girls with their new stepsisters."

"Where would you go, alone, at Christmas?" She asked the question without thinking, but she understood Christmas could be hard for some. Heck it was still hard for her with her mom gone.

"My parents have a place in Mexico. I could go there, but now, I want to be here. I'll invite them up if I can get a guest bedroom painted in time."

"I'll do it for you. Consider it a Christmas gift," she said with a smile, feeling sunny and light at the idea of the holiday this year. "I'll squeeze it in."

"Thanks, but I'll get my mom to pick the color and the window dressing. She can order furniture if she wants. Your priorities will keep you busy enough."

"Okay, but the offer stands," she said.

"What about you?" He asked. "What are your plans?"

She smiled with a light laugh. "I'll be with the boys, of course. We'll have their favorite breakfast which includes bacon. It's a treat. Then we'll watch a movie or two before I cook their favorite dinner." Christmas would be so much better than last year, when she was torn about what to do and where to go when she quit her job.

"So, not a turkey dinner?"

"When you're three it's tough to stretch your preferences to grown up turkey and mashed potatoes. But I'll bake a pie for dessert. They're a big hit." She planned on introducing the boys to holiday meals gradually. And once she could afford all the trimmings, of course.

She was still on a tight budget because she wanted to move and that would take money. The boys would get one fun gift each and some new clothes that were actually new and not from a thrift store. She was on the way, but she needed more work lined up so her budget could stretch to a nicer place to live.

She took one last sip of coffee, emptying the mug. Try as she might, she couldn't come up with another reason to stay longer. Being in the room that had consumed her for weeks should bore her, but she loved how the work had turned out. The cabinets, a rich maple color on the bottom with a distressed beige on top were perfectly installed. The countertops were gorgeous marble lightly veined in brown/grey that pulled color from the cabinetry. Max had taken her suggestions for color choices and she loved how well the colors worked. "I see the cleaning you've done."

"I'll get the top cabinets finished when the girls are in bed tonight. The house will be quiet, and I'll work faster alone." He scrubbed his scalp. "I love those two, but wow, do they talk a lot. And when they're talking, they stop moving. The cleaning would take a week if I left them to it."

"To Christmas and new traditions." She held up her mug and he clinked his with hers. Their gazes locked and she smiled when he looked at her mouth.

"Speaking of new traditions. Would you and the boys enjoy walking the path with us? They seem to have fallen in love with my dog."

"And your girls," she said softly, with a significant look out to the backyard. The four children were laughing as the girls swung the boys in circles and the dog leaped and twirled.

The conversation with Karen about the kitchen reminded her of a favor she needed. It was time to remind him that she'd asked a few weeks ago. "Sure, we can take a walk. But then I'm off to Good Value and the gas station."

Chapter Thirteen

The four children ran ahead, although Willow would hate that her father lumped her in with the three younger kids. Jackson strained at his leash to catch up to them. "I don't remember Rex pulling on his leash this way when I was a kid." He frowned and stopped walking to pull the dog back. "Heel," he said in a stern tone which the dog ignored. Instead of sitting at heel, he whined and pulled harder.

Kaylin grinned. "I'm sure your parents trained him before giving you the leash."

He felt sheepish. "Yeah, I guess they did." Jackson had behaved like a perfectly trained dog earlier. But now he tested Max's patience. "Karen had Jackson under control and now he's being a jerk. I don't have a clue what I'm doing wrong."

"Call Karen. I'm surprised she didn't give you more instruction before she left."

"The meet turned into a circus when you and the boys arrived. Not a good time to teach me about an energetic dog. I don't know how much I would've taken in."

"You recognize your shortcomings, that's a good first step. Most men don't. At least, not in my experience."

He gave her a side-eye. "You must know a lot of arrogant men," he commented, wondering which ones in her life had been too proud to ask questions and learn. Her ex? Her father? Both? "Don't assume I'm another one."

"Okay. You're so confident with renos that I assumed you'd know about dogs, too."

"I had Rex. One laidback lab cross. And I wasn't responsible for training him." Jackson was active and stronger than he looked. The girls were already in love. "I'll call Karen for lessons."

They walked in companionable silence for a few yards and Jackson settled into a meander as he sniffed his way along the path.

"I need a favor." She held up her hands looked guilty. "I mentioned it a few weeks back, but now that I see the way the work turned out, it's time to plan."

"Your showcase?" He'd almost forgotten about it.

"Yes. An open house at your place for your neighbors." She waved both arms to include the entire block of homes. "If they see the finished kitchen, they'll be more apt to hire me for jobs at their houses. When I was door knocking, I got a look at some of the properties. People here are aging, and it shows in their homes. Verandas need repair. Windows need caulking or replacing."

He'd noticed that, too. "Those things were part of the reason I liked this street so much. Folks will age out and new people will make improvements. House values should rise."

"Exactly, but in the meantime those older people need to keep up with maintenance. I can do that for them. It would help if the people I spoke with could see my work."

"Of course. Next weekend soon enough? The girls won't be here. Taylor and Brody can come along and entertain Jackson in the backyard. How long will you need?"

"You mentioned two hours the last time we talked about this."

"No problem."

"I figure if even five of the nearby homeowners walk through that will help get the word out. They'll tell their neighbors and friends."

"I'll be around if there are any questions for me."

A streak of stubbornness crossed her face at his offer.

He held up a hand to forestall her. "The neighbors are older, as you said, and sometimes seniors want to hear things from a man. It's wrong, but it's a fact of life with some older people."

She snapped her lips closed. After a moment she spoke again. "You're right. Thanks. Plus, you're the homeowner and a satisfied customer." She nodded. "I have to play to my market. Since you're paying for the work, they may want to hear about my rates anyway. That's better coming from you."

"You can bet they'll tell neighbors on the block about the kitchen and mudroom you did. That bathroom is practical and handy. They may want one on their main floors, too. Old houses weren't built with extra bathrooms."

She gave him a grateful look that made her appear young and naively happy. A burden had shifted off her shoulders and her demeanor lightened.

"Thanks for everything, Max." She blinked and looked to the river, burbling along beside the walkway. "You've been great."

"Speaking of thanks and you still owing me for having the boys while you were away," he said cautiously. "I'm cooking Thanksgiving dinner tomorrow," he said. "My ex-wife and her new family are coming."

Kaylin cocked her eyebrow at him. "You're a few weeks early."

"Canadian Thanksgiving is in October." He shrugged. "This way, we keep our tradition and next month it'll be Cade's family Thanksgiving. Besides, I want to test out my new appliances and kitchen." He nodded. "Aside from understanding next to nothing about dogs, I'm not too sure how to do a whole Thanksgiving meal."

"Your ex will help." Kaylin suddenly looked skittish.

"Before she met Cade and got married, I'd be invited to Karyn's place to be with our girls. I helped like any other guest, but I need to step up here." He blew out a breath. "I can't ask Karyn to cook. I may not know much, but I know it'll take hours. And it's my weekend. I want to try." He'd be hosting one holiday meal a year and he needed to manage it. But this first time loomed. "If I screw this up, I may never get another chance to host. And our Canadian Thanksgiving will disappear."

KAYLIN LOOKED AT WILLOW. "Your daughters?" Although she knew the answer, she had to ask. "Can they do it?"

Max shook his head. "They'll help, but this is on me. As it should be. Obviously, there are some things I can cook, but getting several dishes ready at the same time? All those sides for all those people? I doubt I can do it."

At least Max was aware of the crazy ballet that occurred between pulling out the turkey and making the gravy. When one thing was done, something else had to happen at the same time. Even warming the buns in the oven at the right time was crucial.

"Oh. I see *why* you need help," she said wryly. "I don't believe it should be me."

His lips crimped and she read acceptance in the lift of his shoulders.

But—and it was a big but—she'd asked for a favor and he'd generously given her more time for the open house than she'd asked for. Plus, she could bring the boys for the open house. Max had kindly offered to stay and chat with people who'd prefer to talk with the homeowner. He'd been more than generous with her and she owed him big for taking the boys when she'd been desperate to get to Arizona.

She couldn't say no, though it was a terrible idea.

Willow, Lilly, Taylor, and Brody chased each other farther along the trail. Jackson whined, wanting to join them. The boys' excited giggles drifted back to them. But seeing them only emphasized that Thanksgiving dinner was a big deal for a new family settling in together.

Was she the only one who could save Max's Thanksgiving?

Probably.

Still. "You can find recipes online," she offered. "There are videos you can follow along with."

"I guess," he said doubtfully. And then he hung his head, trying to look helpless. She bit her lip to stop herself from laughing. "If you teach me, I'll never ask you to help with this again."

She bit her lip. Playing with his new dog was one thing, but Willow and Lily deserved to have Thanksgiving be for their new family. No way should she and her boys intrude. "Willow and Lily want you and their new family. They don't want me and the boys there."

"So...you're saying Taylor and Brody won't want to come back to see Jackson tomorrow." He didn't ask, he stated a fact.

Kaylin pinched the bridge of her nose, but she looked past him toward the children. "It's a bad idea, this getting too familiar. Once this project is over, we won't be seeing each other. We won't think of each other or want to be friends. But my boys will miss you and now your big, goofy, happy dog has stolen their hearts, too." This wasn't the time or place for a conversation that swung between their professional relationship and personal one. It was a mistake to be here.

"You don't need to come." He wore a serious expression. "I put you on the spot. It was an impulse. Blame it on the fun time the kids are having; the nice day, the sunshine, whatever. I'm sorry."

"Okay. You're forgiven, but I'm still not coming over." She looked out at the river rushing by and felt the pull of the inevitable. She bit her lip to stop from admitting she'd already changed her mind.

Chapter Fourteen

C *anadian Thanksgiving*

    At nine a.m. Kaylin knocked on Max's door. In her hand was a spiral-bound notebook stuffed with loose pages of recipes and tips for cooking for a large group. The boys were quietly excited about surprising Max. They both held their breaths so as not to screech and give the surprise away.

Max opened the door, his stern expression ruined by the frilly apron he wore. His eyes widened at first sight of her brandishing her notes like a magic wand.

"I'm here to save your Thanksgiving," she announced.

"Yay!" Tayler and Brody yelled as they zoomed by her. "Jackson!" they squealed. "Lily! Willow!" Jackson barked a greeting and skittered across the floor when he took a corner too fast.

Mayhem. Happy, happy mayhem.

"What are you? My fairy godmother?" Max chuckled, looking relieved at her announcement. He opened the door wider.

"Exactly," she said as she shouldered past him into the house. She waved the book high over her head as she strode to the kitchen. "This book was my mother's and it'll help us both. I've never done a big dinner, either."

But when she got to the kitchen, she saw that Max seemed to have things under control. She spun and faced him with her eyes narrowed. "You don't need my help."

He flushed. "Wrong. I looked up how to cook a turkey and got it ready. But it's too early to put it in the oven."

"How big is it?"

"Twelve pounds."

"Good! That's the size my mother used to cook, so her recipes will work for this size group." She hoped. "She used to make a delicious green bean casserole."

"Okay, so should I put this bird back in the fridge?"

"For now." She dug in her oversized purse and pulled out a cake mix. "I should have time to make this before we start cooking the turkey."

"Dessert! I totally forgot about dessert." He grinned. "Thanks."

"My mom was not a woman who took the hard way. We always had cake from a mix." She pulled a container of frosting out of her bag, too, relieved that he seemed okay with the plan.

THREE HOURS LATER, the turkey was ready to go into the oven, the boys had come in for snacks, and Max watched Kaylin sprinkle tiny bits of walnut on top of her freshly frosted cake.

"What's next?" Max asked, studiously not watching as Kaylin's pointed pink tongue stuck out to touch the top of her lip as she focused on keeping the walnut bits even. "Looks delicious," he said. "And smells better than delicious."

She pulled back and lifted her happy face to his. "Thanks. A spice cake with cream cheese frosting and walnuts on top. It was a tradition in our house."

"Not pumpkin pie?" He asked because he had called the bakery to keep one aside for him.

"Well, yes, that, too. But I've never made one and I didn't want store bought."

"What about bakery bought? Because I've got one waiting for pick up at the Welcome Bakery."

Her eyes became circles of delight. "Perfect. It's nice to offer two desserts. Good call."

"I wish you'd reconsider and stay for dinner."

"No way. But I'll let you keep some leftovers for me. How's that?"

"Okay, great." But he wasn't happy with her continued refusal to stay. She insisted she didn't want to intrude on their family time.

The boys ran off to play hide and seek in the house, telling the girls where they were hiding. Their giggles drifted in from the living room, where Max had drywall stacked. Perfect hiding places for three-year-olds.

"Look, Max," she said on a long-suffering sigh. "It's a bad idea for us to meet your ex-wife and her husband. It's too personal. You wouldn't invite Jamie to meet them."

"Right. I wouldn't."

"They'll get the wrong idea and then Willow and Lilly will pick up on that and you'll never get them to stop pestering you about me."

"You're right again, but it still seems wrong not to feed you after you've gone to this much trouble."

"You're saving us leftovers."

"There won't be a lot left." He reached for his keys on the rack over the built-in desk on the far wall. "I'll be back soon."

"I'll be here," she said with a smile to send him on his way. She reached into the fridge and pulled out a bag of fresh green beans. Perfect! Her mom's recipe for her green bean casserole sat on the open notebook on the island and fluttered from the breeze of her movement. "Mom," she said softly, "I wish you were here with me. I wish you'd seen the boys."

The recipe fluttered again and then slipped off the counter and floated to the floor, face up. Kaylin blinked as she bent to pick it up. She missed her mom so much. Some days more than others and helping Max prepare for his Thanksgiving was one of the worst days so far. Usually she told herself she had bigger problems than grief and she could set it aside. Mostly, that worked.

But slowly her problems were melting away. Soon, she'd be able to pay Candace for daycare, and pay more for rent in a nicer place. She already had a date set up for the open house she planned. After that, she saw smooth sailing workwise.

Her career would be up to her, no one could ruin her if she were in charge. But the smaller her worry pile became the more room she had in her heart for grief. She sighed and thought about her mom and how she'd lived her life.

How she'd said a woman had to go for what she wanted. Be the woman she wanted to be. "Grab life," she'd say, "because no one will hand it to you."

Kaylin rinsed off the beans and snapped the ends and tails to clean them. After she found a casserole dish that must have been a hand-me-down from Max's mother, she gathered the rest of the ingredients from the pantry. Max had done a good job getting supplies. Some of the things like spices for baking had probably been suggested by his ex-wife. Most single men didn't have cinnamon and vanilla in their cupboards. She found the ingredients she needed and returned to the kitchen.

Max returned as she completed her dish. "Two pies?" she asked when he set them on the countertop.

"I can't send you and the boys home without a pumpkin pie."

Grab what you want, came a voice inside her head that sounded like her mom's.

"Thank you," she said simply, and kissed him.

Lightly, at first. A mere brush of her lips against his. The brush made something female rise inside her chest. Max looked startled but she wanted more than this butterfly kiss. With their lips separated by half an inch, she made her decision.

Kaylin moved in for a second kiss even though Max still looked stunned. Her heart thudded hard and the female thing that had risen wanted the male in Max to accept he'd been kissed and not just thanked for the pie. Female to male, her lips again found their mark and the feel and taste of him was sweet and hot and yearning. Her eyelids drifted closed as she assuaged the feminine want inside her.

Max pulled back after too short a moment. His breath washed over her lips and she wanted to draw it in. To taste it.

But this was not the time to explore these feelings.

"Kaylin, this is way beyond our boundaries," Max's voice rasped and she'd swear she heard desire under his words.

"Is it? Maybe our boundaries will move someday." She turned back to rinsing potatoes and hummed tunelessly to let him know the conversation was closed.

"Maybe someday," he said and moved to put the pies in the fridge.

He'd tasted of coffee and vanilla and she wondered if he'd had a drink and treat at the bakery. The thrill of kissing him resonated through her muscles, sinew, and bone and made her heart thrum to a heavy beat.

She peeled the potatoes while he cleaned carrots for a dish his mother used to make. He video chatted with her while Kaylin stayed out of the frame. No way would she want his mom asking about her.

Then a suspicion rose. When he finished talking with his mother about her candied carrot dish, Kaylin said, "You could've video chatted with her this whole time. She'd have directed you when you're getting things together for the meal later."

He flushed. "I never thought of that."

"I think you did." Something warm oozed inside her chest. Max wanted her here. And he'd wanted the boys here, too. Of course, he'd been asking her to stay out of politeness, but this was beyond being thoughtful.

He'd wanted his family to know she'd been here. And Max was letting her know she was not a secret. He wanted her in the light.

MAX TOOK HIS CUE FROM Kaylin and pretended the kisses hadn't happened. The first one may have been a quick thanks for the pie, but then for the next one she'd kicked up the intensity and he'd nearly lost his composure. What if he'd let loose and kissed her back?

He stuck his head in the fridge and looked around for something, anything, to pull out. "Should I get the pickles out yet?" Inane question, but it was out there now.

"It's too soon," came her reply. "They're better chilled."

He pulled them out anyway. Then, he moved to the glass-fronted cupboards and found his grandmother's crystal pickle dish. He filled it and slid the dish back into the fridge under Kaylin's watchful eye.

"Good idea." Her bland remark was accompanied by a glance into his eyes that stalled his heart.

"I want you to stay."

She shook her head. "It's not the right time. But soon."

"Soon." He nodded his acceptance because he couldn't force the issue. They were adults and past the awkwardness of the first flush of attraction. "I'd never do anything to—"

He was cut off by the sound of his daughters' voices and Taylor and Brody squealing in welcome.

"Who do we have here?" came a man's voice.

"Max?" It was Karyn calling through the house. Happy little girl voices oohed and aahed about Jackson.

The whole crew had arrived at least an hour ahead of schedule. Kaylin looked wildly around the kitchen as if she could discover a door to another dimension if she only stared hard enough.

"In here," he called.

Karyn breezed in, her mouth smiling wide, looking as if she had something to say. She slammed to a halt at first sight of Kaylin. "Now, I see where the boys came from. Taylor and Brody, right? We've heard so much about them, and you," she said briskly. She held out her hand in greeting. "Kaylin, right? I'm Karyn, Willow and Lily's mom."

"You're early," Max said, trying like hell not to scare Kaylin off. He hoped she didn't think he'd planned this ambush.

"Willow texted us to come now," she explained.

Kaylin drew in a deep breath and took Karyn's hand. Her smile was tremulous, but Karyn's warmth seemed to put the younger woman at ease. "Nice to meet you," she said. "Your daughters are lovely young women. They've been wonderful with my twins."

Karyn rolled her eyes. "They're at an age where half the time I could throttle them but the other half I see the women they'll become. Still, it's nice of you to say." She looked at Max and held up a covered dish. "I came early to see if you need help. And I've brought your favorite green bean casserole."

Kaylin gave him a side-eye.

Chapter Fifteen

She never should have kissed Max, Kaylin thought as she gathered the boys an hour later. As she turned to say goodbye, she felt awkward leaving. Max, Karyn, and Cade had invited her and the boys to stay, but they didn't belong in the midst of this family. These people, this new family needed to establish their celebrations as they learned to blend. "I pitched in because Max was so excited about hosting," she explained. "But I have plans for the rest of the day."

Karyn, who had Cade's youngest daughter glued to her leg, looked softly understanding of Kaylin's awkward excuse and patted her shoulder. "Of course, we're a lot to take in at once. But before you go, I want to say what a great job you're doing here. I love that you helped Max choose the cabinets. He'd have gone too dark if left on his own."

"Thank you," she said quietly.

Cade turned from talking with his other two beautiful girls in the living room. "I want to give you my card, Kaylin. I like what you've done here." He passed her a card that she slipped into her pocket for later. "Call me if you find yourself between jobs. We've always got room for someone as talented as you."

Immediately, she pulled the card back out of her pocket and stared at it. "You're with Fontaine Custom Homes?" His name appeared under his title of Project Manager.

Cade nodded. "Like I said, we have room for people with your eye for detail."

Max grinned. "She's super fussy. Sometimes a pain in the—well, you get the idea. But she's right in the end."

Heat rose in her face at the compliments. They didn't have to be this nice. "I have a great helper in Jamie Hughes."

Cade nodded. "There's room for him, too."

Taylor tugged on her hand. "Mommee, I don't wanna go."

She looked at him and saw a tantrum brewing in his eyes. She took his hand. "I'd best get a move on before this one blows up. Thanks for the card. I'll be in touch," she said quickly and hustled the boys out the open door before she second-guessed her decision to leave.

Kissing Max had been a mistake. Definitely. A great, big, delicious, hot mistake. But she couldn't regret it, because before he pulled away, he'd kissed her back. A twitch of his lips, but still, it was something.

On the other hand, Max felt that dating her was breaking the rules of employee/employer relationships. But she'd been harassed before and she knew the difference. She felt no pressure from him to do anything she didn't want to do. And besides, the kiss had just happened. *On her mom's urging. Sure, blame a woman gone for nearly four years.*

At least she'd been the one to do the lip press. She didn't want Max blaming himself. Clearly, the man was irresistible. She grinned all the way to the Welcome Bakery. Yes, she had the pumpkin pie that Max had bought for them, but it was time to give the boys a treat. They'd been so good today; they'd made her proud.

For the first time since moving here, she felt as if she could afford to take the boys out. The bakery smelled of warm, yeasty bread and fresh-baked pies. There were high stools at a bar against the front window where lone diners could sit and watch the world go by as they sipped coffee, tea, or had a sandwich or slice of pie.

Farther in, she saw a display counter only half full of pre-made sandwiches, rolls, scones of every description and pies and cakes. The display was on the left with a cash register at the end where a woman who must be Candace's mother stood. The other side and back of the bakery had booths for couples or foursomes.

"Taylor and Brody, you go sit there," she pointed at the nearest empty booth. "And don't get up. I'll bring your treats to you." She'd get them each a slice of apple pie. She must have hit a lull in traffic because she was the only person at the counter. "I'll have two slices of apple pie, please. And for myself, coffee and a cheese scone." Her mouth watered at the rich, orange cheese drizzled through the pastry.

"You must be Kaylin if they're the twins I think they are." The woman's beautiful lilting accent rolled over her tongue and into the world, bringing warmth and cheer.

"You're Candace's mother." Kaylin recalled her name was Alyce and she was famous for more than her pies. "Your daughter says you make a wonderful Jamaican Sweet Potato Pudding."

"Candace loves my pudding. And she's told me about her new friend with the beautiful boys."

Kaylin flushed with pride while Alyce looked pleased.

"Welcome to the Welcome Bakery, my dear. And I'd be happy to cut a piece of pie into two if that would suit your boys. Our pieces are generous." Her smile widened. "I serve my pudding with whipped cream."

"I've have some, then. Thank you." She could get a cheese scone another day. She loved trying new desserts.

Alyce reached into the display case and pulled out an individual ceramic cup of brown cakey looking pudding and the apple pie. She cut a wedge of apple pie into two and then covered the pie and the pudding with whipped cream. Alyce put the pie plates and the cup of pudding on a tray. "We don't have table service, but since your boys are being so good, I'll bring over your coffee." The curious glint in the baker's eye said she wanted to chat.

Taylor and Brody bounced with delight in their seats when she walked toward them balancing the tray of treats. "Yummy!"

They went to grab at their pie plates before she set the tray down. "No, wait until it's on the table. I'll hand you your plates."

"Okay," they said in tandem and slumped into their seats.

It gave her a visceral thrill to buy them this treat. It had been a long time and the joy of it created a spurt of salt wash in her eyes. She blinked to clear it.

She settled into her side of the table and used her spoon on the pudding. The flavor was rich and buttery with the perfect number of raisins and enough other pieces of dried fruit to make it interesting. The whipped cream topping added to the taste. *Heaven in a ceramic bowl.*

The boys were silent as they attacked their desserts.

Her thoughts turned to the family gathering she'd just left. What would Willow and Lily think if they knew she'd kissed their father? They seemed to like her, but children could be a minefield when it came to their parents dating. And kissing...and the rest of it. She warmed down to her toes.

Her flush must've shown on her face because when Alyce set a mug of hot coffee in front of her, she clucked her tongue. "I don't believe I want to pay a penny for those thoughts," she said gently. "Any woman mooning the way you are has it bad, my dear."

Kaylin straightened in her seat. "I'm not mooning. There's no one to moon over." The next move was Max's. She would not initiate another kiss. If he chose to ignore it, so be it. If he chose to explore more, then she'd welcome the chance.

"Candace tells me you haven't been in Welcome long, but you visited as a girl?"

"Yes, my Aunt June and Uncle Mack lived here."

"I remember them."

They chatted for a bit about recent news and that her aunt and uncle would stop in to say hello over Christmas. After Alyce returned to work, Kaylin felt rattled that her pre-occupation with Max was noticeable.

She finished her pudding and was coaxing the boys to finish their milk when a male voice hailed her. Turning her head, she saw Logan Hughes stepping up to the table.

"Hi, Kaylin." He held up a bag. "I grabbed dessert for Elle and me. It's date night and our only secret treat."

"With all those children, I guess a sneak treat is a big thing."

He laughed. "Got it in one." He greeted the boys and asked a few questions about their favorite TV shows and responded with interest.

"You really do understand kids."

"I didn't think I did. I don't have nieces or nephews, but Elle's children drew me in on sight. I never knew how much I wanted a big family until she let me join hers."

"And now you have two of your own. Parenting twins is a lot." She remembered that Elle had two sets, one from a previous marriage and the pair she had with Logan. It wasn't her place to ask if they planned to stop there. She dug into her pocket and pulled out the card Cade Devine had given her. She showed it to Logan. "Have you heard about this builder?"

He looked at the card. "Sure. Fontaine Homes is a good-sized company and expanding. They build custom homes and get work through word-of-mouth. I've recommended them to people who want to downsize but also want more than an average bungalow or condo."

"I sort of got an invitation to talk to them about work."

Logan smoothed his chin. "They work south of here mostly, so you'd have a commute, but they're reputable."

"Thanks, now I have more to think about." Maybe they'd be willing to take her on and get her through her apprenticeship. A licenced electrician made more than she could make working for herself. And she'd have benefits.

But commuting was impossible right now. She couldn't add an hour or more to her workdays. At least not until the boys were in school and could have before and after school care. She tapped the card on the tabletop and thanked Logan for his advice.

He very kindly included Taylor and Brody in his goodbyes and left.

As she shepherded her children outside, she realized that she'd chatted with two people she shared connections with. Returning to Welcome may have been a better idea than it had seemed back in August.

Chapter Sixteen

On Friday, Candace accepted Kaylin's check and squeezed her shoulder in thanks. "Your payment gratefully received," her friend said as Kaylin stepped inside the door at the side of Candace's house. The daycare was on the left at the back of the house and the kitchen was straight ahead. Candace used a front bedroom as a den for TV.

"I'm so grateful you allowed the bartering," Kaylin said with a smile, proud to pay for daycare. "I couldn't have managed without your help." Candace had been extending their barter agreement as more repairs had come up, but Kaylin suspected her friend wanted to help her save for a move to a bigger place.

"It worked out great for both of us." Candace looked pleased and cheery. "My house is fixed up and my faucets aren't dripping. Even my dad said I made a good bargain."

Kaylin closed the door behind her against the brisk late October breeze. The rainy season had begun, and gloom was settling in the sky like a grey wool blanket.

"Taylor and Brody, your mom's here."

There were a couple of other children still playing, so Kaylin didn't feel as if she'd arrived late. She never forgot Candace's need to have her workday end so she could take care of Dayna. That, and the longer commute had been major reasons she hadn't called Cade Devine to talk about a position with Fontaine Homes. She couldn't handle a longer workday and she couldn't ask for longer hours from Candace.

"Aw! We're having fun."

"You'll be back on Monday," Kaylin told Taylor, who hated leaving.

"Do you have time for a cup?" Candace invited. Sometimes on Fridays, Candace welcomed her to hang out for a short while. They caught up on each other's week while their children played.

"Sure. The boys will be happy to play for a while longer. After this, I have errands to run." She was pleased because this month, she wouldn't be forced to say no to Taylor's request for his favorite food. "I'm buying bacon for the boys' breakfast. It's been so long they've probably forgotten what it tastes like."

Candace laughed and waved her to a stool in the kitchen. "So, what's new this week?"

Instead of taking a seat, Kaylin went to the coffee maker. "You sit, I'll get coffee. You've had a busy week." Daycare meant long hours and lots of noise. Kaylin knew where Candace kept everything, and she felt at home in her friend's kitchen.

"To answer your question. There's not much new in my life. I'm avoiding Max." Avoiding may not be the right word, but she wasn't seeking him out. All week he'd acted as if the kisses hadn't happened. They seemed at a standstill. "Anything new with you?"

"Nothing." Candace propped her chin in her hand. "No handsome men to avoid in *my* life."

Kaylin served their coffees and ignored the gentle dig.

"Avoiding Max is self defense," she explained. "Who invites their contractor to help cook Thanksgiving dinner when the day should be about blending two families? Having his children's stepfamily in his home should have been enough. But no, Max thought having us invade that"—she waved her hands in circles— "would be fine? No way." She shook her head vehemently.

"Maybe he needed a buffer with the ex and the new family stuff." Candace held up her hands to forestall any response from Kaylin. "You said he talked about going away for Christmas. By himself." She raised her eyebrows and held her tongue for a moment, but it was clear she had more to say. "And, in the end, you didn't stay for the meal you helped to cook, so they got the family time they needed."

Kaylin waited for the next comment because Candace paced them out.

"Maybe Max wanted emotional support for his first Thanksgiving as host and you were his only option."

Sympathy warmed Kaylin's chest. "I didn't consider that big, strong Max might need emotional support." She frowned. No, that couldn't be right. Could it?

"How will you avoid him during your open house tomorrow?"

"I won't. But it'll be okay. He'll be around to answer questions from the neighbors, but he won't hover. If the rain holds off, he'll keep the boys outside with the dog."

"I FRETTED ABOUT WHAT to wear," Kaylin told Max when he opened his front door to her knock the next morning. The boys zoomed past him and then kicked off their shoes onto the boot tray by the front door. He'd hoped for better weather this morning, but the rain was a gentle mist. Not bad enough to keep the neighbors from coming by, but too wet to keep the boys outside.

"Weather report says we're in for some sunny patches, so that'll help," he offered as he took in her new black jeans and deep purple loose-fitting sweater. *Stunning.* "What's wrong with what you're wearing? You look good." But then she always looked good to him, even with paint smudges on her cheek or drywall dust in her hair.

She flushed and set a bouquet of flowers on the built-in bench seat and then turned away to shed her jacket. He helped with her sleeves, aware of the fruity scent of her shampoo. Her curls were bouncier than usual.

"I went back and forth about wearing a skirt and heels to look professional or looking like a competent contractor. It's important that I look like I can do the work."

"Then you picked the perfect clothes." He never worried about stuff like this; if his tie was straight, he was good to go. But he was a man, so maybe he needn't worry about looking competent because people assumed that he was. He frowned.

"I planned to spend the time in the yard with Taylor, Brody, and Jackson, but it's too wet," he said. "Instead, I'll park the boys in my room with the TV and put the dog in his crate upstairs with them."

"Thanks. I'll check on them when we have a lull." She hung up her jacket in the newly built closet. The bench seat had storage under the seat. Houses from this era didn't have front hall closets or benches so they were a good addition. The living and dining rooms still smelled faintly of fresh paint and looked bright and cheery with the new lighting installed.

He trailed her to the kitchen, trying not to notice how fit she looked in her new, snug jeans. "It smells good in here," she said with a sniff. "Cookies?"

"Out of a tube, but they smell like homemade," he said, absurdly happy she noticed. "I've heard the smell is good for open houses."

She smiled as if the sun had come out on a cloudy day. The smile caught at him and he stepped back. "Thanks for thinking of it."

This was the first time she'd looked him in the eye since she'd kissed him last week.

The kiss that shouldn't have happened. The kiss he desperately wanted to repeat but couldn't. He'd hurt her by not reciprocating, but he'd been surprised and concerned at the same time. So, he'd done the smart thing and backed off.

So had Kaylin.

The bouquet and vase brightened the kitchen and added color. She placed them beside the plate of cookies. There was a fresh-brewed pot of coffee and a kettle ready to boil if someone asked for tea. While she fussed about how everything was placed, he took the boys and the dog upstairs.

The doorbell rang as he descended the stairs, and her open house began. The new front hall closet and bench were a hit as the people two doors down came in.

"Hello, Neighbor," the man said when he saw Max. They introduced themselves as the Alberts and Max led them into the kitchen to meet Kaylin, who greeted them warmly and took over explaining the work she'd done.

"This is a magnificent kitchen. It's perfectly gorgeous," Mrs. Albert said as she smoothed her hand over the countertop and eyed the cabinets.

Kaylin smiled and opened a photo album she'd had printed. "I have the before pictures in here, if you'd like to see them." The Alberts helped themselves to a cookie, accepted a cup of coffee each and pored over the photos. They gave each other significant glances and then looked at Max and Kaylin.

"We've been retired long enough to see wear and tear on our place. Being home during the day, every day, puts the age of the house into perspective. But we're not sure how to freshen it up."

Kaylin nodded and expertly explained some of the easier jobs she could do.

Max left them to it because another woman arrived. She said she lived on the next block and was recently widowed. She wanted to get her home ready to sell.

Declining the offered snacks, Mrs. Gladstone got to the point. "I can see the girl does good work," she said to Max, "but I only want to put lipstick on a pig and get out of here."

She stepped aside as the Alberts left to view the mudroom and bath. Kaylin turned toward Max and the new arrival.

"I hate the gloomy winters," the older woman said with a sour expression. "Now that I'm free to choose for myself, I'm moving to a sunnier climate."

He caught Kaylin's eye and suppressed a grin. She covered a smirk and took the woman to the living room and dining room, where the freshly painted walls brightened the space. "Then you'll want some new paint and your hardwood floors refinished."

"I guess. There's old broadloom down now, but there's hardwood under it. How much?"

Kaylin was the only one who could answer the blunt questions and she took them in stride. She was equally direct and brought a no-nonsense vibe to the negotiation.

Max was amazed with Kaylin's ability with people and by the end of the two hours, she'd lined up several appointments to give estimates.

Kaylin was well on her way to creating her new life for herself and her sons.

Max couldn't be prouder. And on a selfish thought, he realized the sooner she was independent and finished with his house, the sooner he could follow up on that kiss. But until then, they'd go back to being friends they way they'd agreed before the kisses.

BLACK FRIDAY

It was Max's weekend to have the girls, but they wanted to spend it shopping with Karyn. He'd be the worst father ever created if he'd said no. Considering the crush of shoppers they'd have to contend with, he told them to be safe, be smart, and to let go of the clothes if they found themselves in a squabble over a sweater.

He'd spent the previous day at Karyn and Cade's for American Thanksgiving where he'd met Cade's in-laws from his first marriage. They were good people and had bonded with Lily and Willow as soon as they'd met the previous summer. He felt good about how well his girls were doing with their new situation. They'd told him they felt welcome and enjoyed their new stepsisters.

He was beginning to believe Logan was onto something when he'd said more family had been the key to his happiness.

Jackson saw him reach for the leash and the dog leaped and twirled at the sign that they'd be heading out. As much as he loved having the dog, when he was without his kids and there was no reno work being done, this big old house was lonely. He decided he needed to make some noise after their walk so he'd hit the basement and put up a couple of sheets of drywall.

It seemed everyone else was spending time with family. He hunkered into his rain slicker and pulled up the hood. It was a wet day again, but Jackson never minded, and they needed the exercise. A good poodle was a tired poodle, but it seemed the dog had endless energy.

He imagined Kaylin and her boys were enjoying their time together. He was pleased with the progress on the house and could see the end result taking shape. She'd been smart to do a quick paint job in the living and dining rooms in time for her open house.

According to Jamie, she'd snared at least two projects before Christmas. He hadn't heard the news from her because she was back to avoiding him. Sure, they'd talked and smiled a bit together at the open house and she'd thanked him for his support. There'd been a few questions for him regarding her work ethic and prices, but her work was outstanding, and no one had questioned her ability to get the job done right.

The wet started to get to him by the time they reached the park at the bend in the river. The play equipment looked like a collection of rods and poles and emptiness. Nothing so cold and alone as a play park in the rain without any kids. He averted his gaze. He didn't need the reminder that he felt the same way the play equipment looked.

"Hey, boy, let's jog the walkway. We won't crash into anyone. There's no one else around." With that, he set off, hoping to burn off his blues. *Must be the rain.*

When he returned home forty-five minutes later, he saw a familiar truck parked in front of his house. Kaylin.

He hurried toward home and saw her and the boys waiting, huddled against the brisk wind beside his front door. They were shielded from the rain, but the wind had picked up. "Hi! How long have you been waiting?" The boys cheered and broke away from their huddle to hug the sopping dog.

"Only ten minutes or so. When I didn't hear Jackson bark when I knocked, I assumed you'd taken him for a walk. I didn't think you'd be out long in this weather."

"You should have used your key," he said, giving her a stern look.

"I keep it at home for workdays. I wasn't at home when I decided to stop in unannounced." She faked a guilty look that made him smile.

"Let me get us inside. I'll go in the back door and dry Jackson off with some old towels I keep in the mudroom."

"We'll come with you," she said with a relieved smile. "Sorry for stopping in this way. You probably have plans."

"Only a plan to throw up a couple of sheets of drywall in the basement. Having company is no problem." God, he was glad to see her. And on a day off, too. His mood lightened at the prospect of having some life in the house for awhile.

Pathetic. But he grinned all the way to the back door. Two adults, two excited boys, and a big dog crowded through the door into the mud room. Kaylin closed the door after them.

"Hey," he said happily, "look at this, there's room for all of us." He caught her eye and the silent signal that passed between them said she was pleased, too.

The boys stretched to reach the towels he kept on a shelf for this kind of emergency. Their busy arms and determination to be first to help made it more difficult. Jackson shook rainwater off in sheets and promptly rose to his hind feet and slapped his paws on Kaylin's shoulders in welcome.

The boys screeched with laughter as Kaylin grinned into Jackson's wide smile and lolling tongue. She swayed with him in a dance that had the three males laughing together. "I bet he could do a great rumba," Kaylin quipped.

"Thanks, boys," Max said, "But I'll take it from here." They handed him the towels and he started the wipe down. Jackson seemed to appreciate his efforts. "Good boy," Max crooned.

Meanwhile, Kaylin took wet jackets off the boys and hung them on the hooks she'd insisted Max would need. Taylor and Brody made a competition of how far they could kick off their boots. Taylor won by a hair with landing his halfway into the bathroom.

"Wash your hands, boys," Kaylin said over the din. Both boys groused but dutifully went to use the sink. Kaylin had to lift them so they could reach the faucet and soap dispenser.

"I'll bring a stool in here," Max offered.

"No need, we're okay," Kaylin said on a huff of air as she hoisted the second boy so he could reach.

Still, he'd put a stool in the corner for future use. Max urged Jackson into his crate to dry off and the dog landed with a thump. His eyes rolled with yearning and Max relented. "But I'm drying off your paws a bit more," he muttered as he smoothed a dry corner of towel across each paw. "There, done." To Kaylin, he said, "I don't know about you, but I need something warm." The warmth near his heart didn't count.

"Me, too. Coffee, please."

"I have hot chocolate for the boys." Willow and Lily loved it made with milk.

"Yay!"

Taylor looked up at him, his eyes shining. "You gots marshmallows?"

"Yes, I have marshmallows."

She shuffled the boys into the kitchen, with Jackson squeezing through the doorway with them.

"The dog should probably not shove his way in with us," Max said, "but I never think of stopping him until it's too late." And, since Jackson was part of the family, Max didn't have the heart to make him believe otherwise.

His guests settled at the kitchen island on stools while he made coffee and hot chocolate.

"I saw an apartment this morning," Kaylin began.

"Good," he said and settled his hand against the counter's edge.

She lifted one shoulder. Dropped it. "That's sort of why I showed up on your doorstep. Everyone in town is busy with family today."

"Or shopping," he pointed out. She'd come by because she expected he'd be alone. Nice. Or it showed how lonely she thought he was.

"I wanted to talk to another adult about the place I saw," she explained. "I rented where I am now because of the price but this feels more important now that boys need more than a bed and a roof overhead."

"Tell me," he urged her, pleased that she'd come to him.

"It's in a low-rise building built in the 1950s. There's a balcony and it's on the second floor, so I won't always need the elevator."

This sounded like a nice step up from the dump she was living in now. "Not to put a damper on things, but can you afford to pay more?"

She flushed, very prettily. "Thanks to you paying me for any extra I do, yes I can. And I can't keep the boys in that dark pit any longer. It's not healthy."

Which confirmed his own thoughts about the basement unit. That day he'd driven past was etched in his mind. Old, cramped and damp, were the adjectives he'd use to describe what he'd seen.

"The second floor would be good. They won't be able to walk outside into the parking lot or anything." Unless these two monkeys decided to try climbing down. But he didn't think she'd want to hear that thought.

"It's two bedrooms so they'll have their own room, and I won't be sleeping on the sofa in the living room. The appliances are old, but they work. The building's clean and in good repair. Apparently, the last tenant lived in the unit for years before going to live with her daughter."

"That's a good sign. Does the landlord live in the building?"

"Yes." She smiled and blew out a huff of breath. "I needed to say this out loud. It's good, right?" Kaylin asked, uncharacteristically hesitant.

"It sounds great. Where is it?"

"It's one block behind Main Street on Second Avenue. So, two blocks over that way." She waved a hand to indicate the space behind her.

Because of the curve near the park, Cross street ran parallel with Main and Second also paralleled Main. "That's close. You'll be able to walk the boys to the park." He'd probably see them there. Occasionally.

Kaylin pulled a colorful box out of her purse. "I went to a dollar store and picked this up. I thought it could keep them busy for a few minutes." She set the puzzle box on the countertop and the boys cheered while he poured their drinks. "When you finish your hot chocolate, you can put this together on the living room floor," she told them. More cheers.

Max had to turn way to pour their mugs of coffee and he needed the moment to think. She and the boys would live nearby. He'd be seeing them around the neighborhood. Frequently, if he had any say in it.

And there it was...he wanted Kaylin and her boys in his life. He wanted her living nearby. Wanted to see her boys playing at the park and then learning to ride bikes on the pathway.

This attraction he felt for her wasn't a passing interest. They were past the age of flirting or playing games. She'd kissed *him,* and if that wasn't a sure sign of a woman's interest, he didn't know what was.

They had a chance here. A real chance. Everything inside him stilled as he let relief and desire roll through him. He wanted this chance with her.

"I offered to paint the apartment to cover the damage deposit to save on cash," she said. "The landlord seemed pleased with the idea."

He glanced over his shoulder. "Good idea. But can you squeeze it in between here and your other jobs?"

"I'll pay Jamie to do it. He's fast and cheaper than the damage deposit."

It made sense. The rush of annoyance he felt at Jamie being the one to help her out bothered him. He wanted to be the man she asked. But he couldn't speak up about it. Not yet.

"And he likes kids and keeps the swing set and slide in good condition."

Max struggled to keep up because she was still talking about the landlord and he was stuck thinking about Jamie. *Get a grip.*

"It's not much, but Taylor and Brody can burn off some energy right outside on the back lawn. There are other children in the building because I saw strollers and toys on the balconies."

He swung back to face her. "They'll have friends in the building," he said with a nod.

She smiled widely back at him and their gazes locked as her good fortune washed over them both.

He took a deep breath and spoke without thinking. "What do you say we head over to the store this afternoon so you can help me pick Christmas decorations for the house?" He didn't want their visit to end. "I need new lights and whatever else will look good on the lawn."

The smile that broke over her face at his suggestion made his heart thud. Uh-oh. Kaylin was beautiful. "I'd love that," she said fervently, a flush highlighting her cheeks.

"Great. After we've had our drinks and the puzzle's been put together, we'll go. You can show me the building on the way."

Chapter Seventeen

Max followed Kaylin's truck to the apartment building. When they pulled to a stop across the street he climbed out and walked to where she sat inside her truck, staring at the place.

"I'm impressed at how tidy the building and grounds are."

"Yes, me, too," she responded happily.

Well-maintained and clean, the building was a gem. One street over from Main, the low-rise sat behind a wide lawn with a playground on the side. "You don't see this kind of room on a manicured lot in a new building. It's homey."

"Yes," she said with a gusty sigh. "Homey is exactly right."

"Let's head to the bakery for lunch," he said loudly enough for the boys to hear. Kaylin raised both eyebrows. The boys whooped and cheered and put an end to whatever protest their mother might make.

Shorty after, they were settled in a booth for four. The boys shared a ham and cheese sandwich and he and Kaylin discovered a mutual love of Alyce's cheese scones. For dessert they ordered a whole apple pie so Kaylin could take the remainder home. Alyce herself delivered the pie to the table with a cardboard pie box for Kaylin.

Kaylin smiled widely. "Thanks, Alyce."

"Oh, you're welcome my dear. I'll say hello to Candace for you." Her cheery smile didn't quite hide the curiosity in her gaze.

As soon as Alyce was out of earshot, Kaylin leaned across the table. "Now the gossips in town will know we came here. We should have gone for burgers at a drive-through."

"How have you missed the part where we're both newcomers and no one will care?"

She looked relieved. "You're right. Nobody knows us."

"Besides, I don't want to miss out on this pie. No way. And I have nothing to hide. We're single parents, way past the age of consent and...well, that's it." Her eyes were wide and serious by the time he finished his speech.

"Max," she whispered. "The work will be finished soon, and I'll be doing other projects. Maybe we should have waited until then."

"If you feel that you don't have a choice here, say so now."

"I have a choice," she said and pulled back briskly. "And I choose to be here with you."

"Good. Then, we'll take it easy and see where this goes. There's no rush or pressure on either side."

"Right. No rush. No pressure. We can do this kind of thing now and again. Spend time with the boys. Easy and casual."

He nodded. This was a good place to start. She was interested and cautious, like him. "By the way, I haven't quit thinking about that kiss."

"I'm glad," she said primly. "You weren't meant to." She glanced to the side. "Brody, don't you dare throw that at your brother."

Max had been so caught up in their conversation, he'd forgotten they had two little boys sitting across from each other. "Next time, we seat them on opposite corners, so it's harder to start something." But he was laughing as he said it and feeling light and...hopeful.

NEXT TIME. Kaylin repeated Max's words to herself. She smiled at the easy assumption Max had made. But, considering he hadn't forgotten their kiss...

For one-stop shopping they each drove to the big box hardware and home store. Taylor and Brody squealed with excitement when he saw the big square orange sign above the entrance. "I wanna ride on Max first!" he yelled.

"Nah! Momma, I wanna go first," his brother hollered.

"Poor Max," she said on a sigh. But as she watched him approach the car, he looked windblown and happy. So happy.

She grinned back at him. Today felt like family fun without the pressure of dating. It had been years since she'd dated, and she felt out of touch with the scene. Max always seemed to know what to say to make her feel good and "No, rush. No pressure," had been the best possible thing to hear.

She waited patiently while the boys undid their car seat chest clips, but they needed help pressing the stiff button on their lap clips. By the time she'd got Brody undone, Max had helped Taylor. It felt odd sometimes to have help with the boys, but other times, like this, she felt grateful.

With the twins out of her truck and each holding hands with an adult, they crossed the parking lot. "You were right about the apartment building. It's a good-looking place to call home," Max told her.

"It reminds me of a building I grew up in," she admitted. "There aren't a lot of them so tuned into the young children that live there." She'd felt nostalgic on first sight and hadn't needed his approval, but she felt glad that he saw what she did in the older building.

"Taylor and Brody," he said in an announcer's voice. "I will need your help to pick my lawn decorations for Christmas." He clapped his hands once to command their full attention.

"Lights and Santa!" said Taylor.

"Reindeer!" added Brody.

"How about we look at the blow-up figures and decide then?" Max asked with a laugh in his voice.

"Yay!"

AN HOUR LATER, ONE box containing a portly Santa on his sleigh, one box that held a blow up bag of toys that Max planned to set next to the Santa, as per Taylor's instructions, 50 strings of lights, and one free-standing Rudolph with a brightly lit nose that Brody had pointed out, filled their flat deck cart. Kaylin pushed a large cart filled with indoor decorations like wreaths and garlands for wrapping around the staircase railing and a couple of boxes that contained Christmas themed dishes and serving platters. He wasn't convinced he needed them, but she was adamant Christmas should fill the house, even the kitchen cupboards. She also had several packages of delicate glass-blown ornaments for trimming the tree.

Max was skeptical about keeping those fancy ones from being shattered, but Kaylin promised to find some unbreakable ones, too.

"We bought so much I'll need to use space in your pickup to get everything home." Max hadn't enjoyed a morning more since he'd moved to Welcome.

Kaylin had both boys by the hand as they waited for Max to pay for his purchases. Taylor and Brody vibrated with excitement. Three was the perfect age for Christmas, he thought, remembering his daughters at that age. Even the cashier grinned along with the twins. The middle-aged woman handed each of them a candy cane from a stash she had in her smock pocket.

A chorus of thank yous rang out and the woman chuckled. "What a lovely family you have," she said to Max with a smile. "Such handsome and polite little boys."

Max frowned. Is that how they looked? He hadn't considered what others would see when they saw him with three-year-olds.

Feeling disloyal to Willow and Lily, he blurted, "I have daughters."

"Oh, sorry," the woman said with an embarrassed glance. She turned back to her register.

"But, yes, these two are very polite," he said, feeling awkward. "Thanks to their mom, here." He waved a hand vaguely in Kaylin's direction.

"I'm a big boy," Taylor announced. "Not a little boy."

"Me, too!"

Kaylin spoke to them. "You can have your candy cane after we unload these packages at Max's."

"Are we going there right now?"

"Yes. And then, we'll see the man you met earlier about renting that new place to live." She didn't look in Max's direction all the way through the parking lot. After she got the boys buckled into their seats, she came to stand beside Max as he tucked the last package of lights inside.

"That was fun." She tucked a lock of hair behind her ear. "I'm stopping by to see the landlord after we get this to your place. I already told him I'd be there this afternoon. Thanks for lunch."

She stalked to her door and climbed in. A moment later, the truck rumbled to life and she pulled out of her parking spot. Max hurried to his SUV and followed, wondering what he'd said that had darkened her mood.

After unloading the new lawn decorations, he piled the boxes on the veranda. Kaylin carried her cargo into the mudroom. He'd deal with those boxes later.

"Care to come by sometime soon to help with the outdoor stuff? The boys can string the lights together and tell me if they're straight after I get them strung." He planned on trimming the house in colored bulbs and to wrap the bare tree limbs on his maple tree with plain white.

He hadn't shared his plan with Kaylin because she was pre-occupied with seeing the new landlord and settling her business there. When she left, she gave him a desultory wave. The exact opposite of the rapid, excited waves that came from Taylor and Brody.

Chapter Eighteen

"D o you have time to talk?" Kaylin asked Candace on the phone after signing her application to rent. All she needed now was word from Mr. Meacham that she'd been approved. She had good references from her previous landlords, and she had signed contracts for more work to carry her through to spring.

He'd been concerned that she didn't have a salaried job like most tenants, but she could see he had a soft spot for the twins and she'd gone into more detail about her marketing plans and business projections than she might have with someone else. "There's some stuff I want to run past you."

"Is it Max stuff?"

"Yes and no."

"Good, I want to talk to you, too. Come on over and pick up a baguette at the bakery on the way by. Oh, and a bag of salad. We'll have supper."

A friend. Kaylin's heart warmed. She hadn't had such an easy friendship in far too long. Her last had been in high school and that had faded because Suze had left for college. Kaylin had had to go to work right out of high school. Suze was a dentist now and had married soon after opening her practice three years ago.

She'd missed Suze but understood how little they had in common now. Life had overtaken them both. They kept in touch on social media, but beyond that, crickets.

"Boys, we're going to see Candace and Dayna and we have two stops to make." She glanced into the backseat to give them her best mommy glare. "Be good in the bakery and in the grocery store."

They howled in rebellion when they heard about the stops.

141

But as it turned out, Candace had left word at the bakery that Kaylin would be in. Along with the baguette, the server handed her a bag of washed lettuce from the cooler. She waved her away from the cash register, saying it was on the house.

"Thank you!" Candace was kind and generous and always knew what to say and how to listen. Valuable traits in a girlfriend.

The children ate quickly for once and disappeared into the playroom. After Kaylin and Candace settled in for a cup of tea after their meal, Candace spoke. "Okay, who's first?"

"Since you complain that you never have news, you go first," Kaylin said happily. From what she could overhear, Dayna was in charge of the tea party in the playroom. "We may need to make this quick. No telling how long they'll be willing to sit at a table playing tea party."

"Jamie Hughes stopped by the other day." Candace deadpanned the announcement.

"He did? I had no idea he had that planned. He said nothing to me."

"You'd have warned me?"

"Probably. It would be the decent thing to do," Kaylin teased. "I want all the details."

"Not much to tell. I waved goodbye to my last kid for the day and when I turned to walk back into the house, I saw him standing at the corner of the lawn, looking at me."

"And?"

"He waved. Kind of nervous, you know?"

"I think he has a hard time reaching out. He keeps to work and his family mostly." From what she'd observed Jamie had no social life. Apart from a natural question about how Candace was doing, he had never mentioned going out or hanging with friends. "He never asked about you again after that time a few weeks ago."

"That's not the Jamie I remember from high school. He was fun and outgoing and the most popular boy in school. He captained the football team, made a name for himself and got a full ride to college." She propped her chin on her hand. "He wasn't for a girl like me. I'm surprised he remembered me at all."

"He remembered you fondly enough to ask about you, so he must've noticed you back then."

"Everyone noticed me because my brother and I were the only bi-racial kids in town. I had lots of girlfriends through school and my brother cut a swath through them, but boys didn't ask me out much."

"Sometimes the real smart girls are overlooked," Kaylin said. "Boys can be intimidated when faced with intellectual superiority."

Candace laughed hard at that.

"I'm serious," Kaylin said. "You're smart and fun and beautiful. I bet boys were tongue-tied around you." From the playroom she heard a complaint about being bored. "Now, let's get back to Jamie."

"I waved back at him and he smiled and asked if he could come up on the porch. We stood outside and talked about people we went to school with and stuff."

"That's it?"

"Yes. That was enough. He told me about his troubles with painkillers and said he was still working hard on recovery. But that it had been nice to talk to someone who remembered him before his troubles began."

"I see. What do you think of all that?"

"I wish him well, of course. But he has a long way to go. Dayna's grandfather had battles that tore his family apart."

"You have Dayna to consider," Kaylin responded in understanding.

"I do. Still, it was nice to catch up with him." Candace poured herself another cup of tea from the pot on the table. "Now, tell me what's happening with Max."

"It's nothing really." She frowned, wondering if she was being too picky. "We were in a check out line today and the cashier assumed we were a family. Max went a funny color when the older woman assumed the boys were his. Then he blurted out that he has daughters and made it clear, very quickly, that the woman was wrong."

"Well, she was wrong." Candace made a face.

"It was disquieting. He's been incredibly nice to Taylor and Brody. Very caring and natural with them. I was surprised by how quickly he denied them. He could have smiled and shrugged it off, but no. He leaped like a scalded cat." It was such a small thing and he overreacted. "I ignored it. Why couldn't he?"

"And you couldn't talk to him with the boys there."

She shook her head. "I'm not talking about this with him. That's why I'm here with you." She raised her eyebrows, looking for sympathy that didn't seem to be coming. "I never considered that he didn't like them, or he'd see them as a bother."

"You haven't dated much as a single mom, have you?"

"I've been too busy with work and chasing Connor for support and avoiding my boss at work until I could do nothing but quit. And then the move to Welcome happened and you know the rest." She wasn't sorry for returning to Welcome, but it had certainly made her life harder than it could've been. Her first weeks here had been rough. "Have I ever said how much it meant to me that you gave me a break on daycare? I couldn't have gone on much longer without your help."

Candace reached across the table and patted her hand. "My mom taught me to watch out for other women, to help when I can, so I recognized desperation when I saw it. But I still drove a hard bargain." One side of her mouth lifted in an ironic grin that brought a smile to Kaylin's heart.

She raised her teacup. "To friends."

"What will you do about Max? You aren't going back to avoiding him, are you?"

"No." Heat rose in her cheeks. Whenever she'd put space between them, she'd missed him, and ended up more entwined. "But I'll guard myself. I won't get my hopes up if he's already looking for a way out."

DECEMBER 5

The next weekend brought sunshine and crisp cold air. Perfect for stringing lights and putting out his decorations, Max decided. Plus, the girls were here to help. Willow and Lily stood beside him surveying the various boxes that contained the decorations he'd purchased with Kaylin and the twins. He looked forward to seeing Taylor and Brody when Kaylin dropped them off.

"Brody and Taylor will be here in a few minutes. Kaylin's running errands and doing a couple of estimates, so we've got them for the morning."

"Great," Willow said. "They can help."

"If you believe that you haven't been around two three-year-olds," he teased. "I imagine we'll be supervising them more than getting lights up." He dreaded being on a ladder with two curious boys on the ground. "Maybe Kaylin can stay awhile after her estimates."

"I'll take them for a walk with Jackson," Lily offered. She sidled up next to him. "How long before the house is finished?"

"Your rooms are next. Are you still happy with the color you chose for the walls?"

"I love it."

Kaylin had called it coral, but it looked like pink to him. Or a shade of light orange, depending on the light. She had jobs lined up through spring and he couldn't be happier for her. Jamie had worked out and had proved to be a self-starter and willing to learn. He and Kaylin had become a great team.

"I'm happy, too," Willow interjected. She had her head in another box and her voice was muffled and distracted. Not one to slack off, Willow liked to get her work done as fast as she could.

"After your rooms are painted, she'll tackle the ensuite bath. That'll eat time because of the plumbing that needs to go in." If they were lucky, they'd find a plumber to work between Christmas and New Year's Eve. Logan had suggested a couple, so Max was hopeful.

When the work was finished, he and Kaylin would make an effort to see each other. There'd be no incidental conversations, or shared cups of coffee at the end of the workday. Making an effort meant planned dates. Dates meant needing a babysitter. He looked at Willow, who was left in charge of Lily if they were alone.

His two daughters, the light of his life. *His children.* The thoughts around them settled into the warmth of love. Willow, steadfast, reliable, and kind. Lily, funny, sweet, and still gangly.

His girls were still adjusting to having three younger stepsisters and a stepdad. They'd moved to a new country, a new home, and new school. Could he ask them to make another adjustment and make room for more people?

He thought of Taylor and Brody. Kaylin's *boys*. Rambunctious, happy, sweet handfuls. From what he'd gleaned from Kaylin, Taylor and Brody had no father figure. The guy was a deadbeat and showed no interest.

It was a lot to consider. Dating Kaylin implied more than friendship. His girls would be watching. Her boys would start to look to him...

This was exactly why he'd decided to avoid women with children. His disappointment with Lindy last year had shown him the many pitfalls. And now, here he was, entrenched in the lives of two boys and their feisty, spectacular mom. He wasn't sure how it happened.

Taylor and Brody were fun loving monkeys, and Kaylin needed help corralling them sometimes. Max had been hands on from the beginning. Literally.

If he hadn't been in the park that day, who knows what might have happened when Taylor had stepped into the road. Max shook his head at the memory. His gut still clenched as he thought about it.

For a guy who didn't want to raise anyone else's children, he'd sure made a mess of steering clear.

But where would this lead? He couldn't see himself going toe to toe with them at fifteen. Teenage boys were a challenge at the best of times, but with a man who wasn't their father things could go bad quickly.

It felt wrong to make Willow and Lily accept more change. He couldn't ask them to fold two more young children into their lives.

As much as he liked Kaylin, things may not work out between them. What if they were attracted because they'd both been lonely and newcomers to town? If that's all it was, then it was doomed from the start. A relationship needed more than fear of loneliness to keep it together.

The questions rolled through his mind, each one complicating what should be a simple one-woman one-man decision.

Max opened a box containing the blow-up Santa that Taylor had liked so much and frowned. Somehow, he'd lumbered into a complicated set of relationships without knowing it.

He and Kaylin. Kaylin and his daughters. His daughters and her sons. He and her sons. And that was only the immediate relationships. What about his ex-wife? Or the boys' father, Connor? Cade and his girls? The question now was: did he want to ease out of these relationships or go all in?

Chapter Nineteen

Kaylin arrived for the house decorating at Max's with two excited boys. "The Santa!" yelled Taylor when he spied Max pulling the blow up out of its box. "Yay! Willow! Lily!"

And as quick as that, Kaylin's heart sank. Again, they were intruding on a special family time. She couldn't remember a specific invitation to help with decorating the house today. At best, there may have been a vague reference when they'd bought everything, but she'd been distracted after that weird turn in the conversation with the cashier.

The other day she'd mentioned that she had estimates to do today and the next thing she knew, she'd agreed to drop the boys off for the morning. Max had offered immediately, and she'd have been a fool to say no.

And now, of course, the weather was perfect for outdoor work and rain free days were rare at this time of year.

Max saw them, gave them a distracted wave, and then turned back to unfolding the large plastic figure while Willow rushed over to help unbuckle the boys. "Hi!" the teen said with a happy smile.

"We're gonna help all day!" Brody screeched in Willow's ear as she worked his lap release.

"I'm sorry, Willow, I'll be back to get them as soon as I can. We don't want to ruin your time with your Dad."

"That's okay," she replied as she helped Brody jump to the ground from the truck.

Kaylin did the same with Taylor and then she walked to Max. "I'll be back in about two hours. Will that be okay?"

"Sure, that's fine," he said as he walked to the packages of light strings. "These will take most of the day anyway." He sounded distracted and why not? He had a full day of work ahead of him.

"See you later, then," she said to him. To the boys she said, "Be good and do as you're told. Don't touch anything you're not supposed to." She held Taylor by the chin to reinforce the directive.

"We won't touch," the twins chorused. She believed they believed, and for the moment, they'd be good. She kissed them both on the forehead and left them.

As she drove and gathered her thoughts about the prospective clients she was meeting today, her phone rang. At a stoplight, she glanced at the screen to see who'd called.

Connor. She should have known it would be him. He was three days late with his support. What excuse would he use this time? When she pulled up in front of her first appointment ten minutes early, she returned his call. No time like the present to ruin her day.

"Hi, you're late again," she blurted the moment he answered.

"You gave me a couple months off, remember? For the wedding?"

"Exactly. That was three months ago." But telling him was useless. Connor would whine that she'd forgotten about the hundred dollars he'd so magnanimously handed over. "And, yes, I remember the money you gave us at the time."

She wouldn't be forced to put up with this much longer. Their expenses plus extras would be covered after she got a few more jobs lined up and completed. Financial independence beckoned like an oasis in a desert.

"I've been watching your progress," Connor said in a sly tone.

That tone never boded well.

"How so?" She asked, suspicion curling through her vitals. She clenched her phone to her ear and scrubbed at her thigh with her other hand.

"You've got a calendar on your site where people book appointments for estimates. That calendar's getting full."

She'd filled some of those days herself to look more in demand. Also, she needed to control her schedule, not be at the whim of looky-loos. But Connor didn't need to be told anything about her life. She'd learned a long time ago that unless it benefitted him, he didn't care what she did.

"My calendar's not full," she declared. "And not every estimate will bring me work." She'd come up with the idea to fill some days when she'd had the open house at Max's, and she'd had to juggle several appointments. "What are you getting at?"

"We're having a kid," he said baldly.

She was stunned. Connor had run off like a teen in a horror flick when they'd learned about the twins coming.

"What does that have to do with your existing sons' support? You'll have three children, instead of two." She put a smile in her voice for this next comment. "I know," she said silkily. "I'll give you their hand-me-downs to help you out. Save you paying for clothes for this new one."

He called her a name she'd heard many times from him before. "You're so successful, you don't need any more of my money," he spat.

His money. "It's money for *your* sons." She hardened her tone. "You be careful Connor. I can afford a lawyer now." She ended the call, wishing she could hurl the cell through the truck windshield.

Just as things were turning around for her, Connor had to pull this. A moment of sympathy for his new pregnant wife washed over her. He'd never change, and the poor woman would learn that any day now.

Kaylin checked her lipstick in the rear-view mirror and slicked a bit of color across them with a shaky hand. She climbed out of her truck, smoothed her hair, her jacket, and then gathered her purse and tablet. This job had suddenly become vital and when she rang the doorbell, she hoped her desperation didn't show in her face.

"Mrs. Baker, I'm Kaylin Simpson." Beside the woman, who appeared to be in her early seventies, stood a man who looked like her son. Kaylin handed him a card as she gave one to his mother.

"This is Gerald, my son," Mrs. Baker explained.

After the pleasantries were over, they walked through the house while Gerald did the talking. A blow hard, she realized. A man who boasted about himself and all he knew about home repair. Kaylin could tell he'd never done most of the things he bragged about.

Mrs. Baker was friendly with neighbors of Max and she'd heard about the work Kaylin had done at Max's house. Gerald was sharp-eyed and skeptical of everything his mother wanted fixed. Price was his only concern. That, and making certain both women understood how skilled he was. *Hah!*

"Will you be here supervising the work, Mr. Baker?" Kaylin asked when they reached the kitchen. His answer, unfortunately, could make a difference to her pricing. She toed at a long strip of torn linoleum that had been taped down with duct tape. Gerald's handiwork, no doubt. The widow needed new flooring in the kitchen.

"This is a tripping hazard," Kaylin pointed out.

"All you need to do is glue it back down," Gerald insisted. "I'll be checking on your work daily, have no fear. This will be done right," he demanded.

"I'll have new," Mrs. Baker told her calmly. "I've already seen some I like."

Every idea Mrs. Baker had for repairs would cost more than Gerald would pay. Her windows need replacing, but he wanted them caulked instead. Her stairs had a loose handrail and he said it was fine as it was.

It was clear that Gerald didn't care about his mother's safety or comfort. Kaylin suspected he wanted to put her in a home so he could sell the house out from under her. Aside from the moment in the kitchen, the older woman had been quietly observant throughout the discussion.

"I'll drop by with my estimate tomorrow morning, Mrs. Baker," Kaylin promised as she left with a wave.

The older woman smiled and winked at her. Kaylin wasn't sure what the wink was for, but she grinned back.

As Kaylin dashed through the canned goods aisle twenty minutes later, she got a call from Mrs. Baker. With an inward groan, expecting the worst, Kaylin answered with a false cheeriness. "Mrs. Baker, how nice of you to call right away. I'm afraid I haven't got the numbers for you, yet."

"My idiot son has left," the widow announced. "I only had him here because he insisted, and I wanted him to understand how bad things have gotten in my house. I'm ashamed to say I believed him these last years when he said he'd come by and fix it up."

"Oh," Kaylin said with caution. "What now? Should I come back?"

"No bother. I recorded the conversation on my phone, so I know what you'll be quoting me on. Email me with the numbers in the morning and we'll get this done."

"If you don't mind me saying so, Mrs. Baker, you sound different." She could hardly believe this was the same woman she'd met today. This Mrs. Baker didn't have a meek bone in her body.

"Gerald put me in a box labeled *decrepit* after his father died. I've given up trying to make him see I'm far from decrepit. Maybe he'll understand now that I'm tired of the life he wants to see me live. I'm in charge, not him."

"I see," she replied. Kaylin heard every word and the nuances. Mrs. Baker was sick of being bullied into accepting the role Gerald had created for her. "I'll get back to you first thing in the morning. I promise. To be honest, I'll need to charge more if I need to take time to explain every step to your son. That kind of thing holds up the work." Handholding a homeowner cost time and money. Money Kaylin couldn't spare.

"He won't bother you. I understand that time is money and arguing with him will waste time." She sighed into the phone.

"Thank you," Kaylin responded, relieved. "And, may I say, Mrs. Baker, you've given me a lot to think about in my own life. Living in a box someone else constructs has its limits."

"You can say that again," Mrs. Baker agreed with a soft chuckle before she hung up.

Connor had forced Kaylin into a role she was tired of playing. Kaylin was cast as the clinging, vindictive ex gouging him for money. A woman bent on stealing his future and ruining his finances.

Connor would never change that view of her and the boys. He was also the kind of man who'd pass bitterness and resentment on to his children.

She had a lot to ponder. What would be best for her boys? To see her wrangling payment from their dad every month while he never wanted to see them. Or letting Connor off the hook so she didn't exhaust herself in the fight? Her energy could be put to better use fighting for her success.

Connor drained her. Sometimes it took a day or two to get his nonsense out of her head. He caused her more sleepless nights than anything else did. He was the one in control and she hated him for it. She worried Taylor and Brody were picking up on her negative emotions.

More importantly, she disliked the person she'd become since having to deal with Connor over their children. Her boys deserved better. They deserved a man who wanted them, who enjoyed their company, who loved them.

Chapter Twenty

As early evening darkened into night, Max stood back enjoying the glow from his light display. The pot-bellied, jolly Santa stood proudly in the quiet rumble of the fan, his spilled bag of toys beside him. The oversized reindeer sparkled from the twinkling lights woven through the wiry white body. The lights that hugged the roof, veranda, and windows would be impossible for Santa to miss on the big night.

Max had Taylor on one hip and Brody on the other. "Ooh, aah," came their hushed voices. "It's pretty," breathed Taylor. "Yeah," whispered Brody.

He bussed each boy on the cheek and set them down. He glanced at Kaylin and saw tears making her eyes glisten. She'd been quiet since she'd returned from her errands earlier. Something had happened to make her pensive. Time to clear the air.

"Willow and Lily take the boys inside for hot chocolate, please. And don't spare the marshmallows."

"We should go," Kaylin said, but the boys were already screeching with cheers and she went unheard except by Max.

"Kaylin, stay for a moment. Girls, we'll catch up," he said.

"Are you making a pizza run?" Lily wanted to know.

"Are we?" he asked Kaylin, who chewed her lip. She shrugged.

"I'll get two," he said and pulled out his phone to order. After they promised pickup in twenty minutes, Max grinned at her. "We have a few minutes of blessed silence," he quipped.

"Because my boys are such a handful? They're too loud and boisterous?" Her voice had an edge he'd never heard before.

"They're normal kids, Kaylin, so yes, they're loud and boisterous." She stood facing him, backlit from a thousand twinkling bulbs, her face shadowed. "What's going on?" he asked.

"Connor's trying to sleaze his way out of child support permanently and I'm going to let him."

"But he's their dad." He'd never understood how a man could walk away.

"He's never been a dad," she muttered bitterly. "Never wanted them. Or me, either, I guess. Now, he's married and has a new baby coming."

"And this means?" He coaxed.

Her shoulders sagged. "I'm tired of fighting him. Tired of trying to make him care. I'm weary to the bone." She covered her head with her hands and locked her fingers together.

"You're letting him off the hook? Taking on his responsibility rather than forcing him to own up?"

"I'm taking back my control," she said clearly, standing straighter and dropping her hands to her hips. She moved so he could see her face. "I'm putting my children first. And I'm making sure they're never hurt like this again."

Something cold slithered between his ribs. "Where does this put us?"

"You know where. If things turn sour between us, our children will suffer. Yours and mine. Go get your pizzas. We'll be gone when you get back." She pressed fingertips to the soft flesh below her eyes. To stem tears?

"I need time to think, Max." She shook her head and hurried toward the house. "I need time."

A LONG TIME LATER, Max made his decision. He and his girls had eaten the first pizza in silence punctuated by unanswered questions.

Willow had asked, "But what did we do wrong?"

He had no answer.

From Lily, came, "This isn't fair. We thought she liked us."

"Me, too," he'd responded.

He washed down his last bite of pizza with the last sip of his beer. He wiped his mouth with his napkin and washed his hands before picking up his phone.

"Are you calling her?" Willow asked as she tossed out the pizza box. "Lily, we should go upstairs."

"I don't want to. I want to know what she says."

His heart clanged as he looked at his daughters. "I'm letting her go. She said she needs time, so I'll give it to her."

"How *much* time?" Lily's voice went high.

His youngest was already anxious. No way would he put her through anything like this again. "That's up to her. We can't force this, Lily. That's not how things work for adults."

Not emotionally mature ones, anyway. Had he subconsciously indicated to Kaylin that he had doubts about being a stepdad? He could think of nothing he'd done to give her that idea, even if he'd been wondering those thoughts this morning.

"But I like her," she whined.

"I do, too," Willow said as she clasped her sister's shoulders from behind. "Come on, Lily. Dad needs to do this alone."

Lily's face crumpled as she leaned back into her sister's embrace. "Okay," she said softly and let Willow lead her out of the kitchen.

Kaylin probably wouldn't answer his call, so he sent a text.

Hey there. I'll finish painting the girls' rms

So U don't have to come in until after Xmas

Have a merry...

DECEMBER 20TH

Max had given her the time she'd asked for. Days and days of it. After she'd left on the evening they'd helped decorate his house, he'd sent her a text saying he would paint the girls' rooms.

The next morning he'd followed up with another text saying he wanted to postpone renovating the ensuite bath to the new year. His next text said they'd make a plan in January for the rest of the work. He'd sent her a smiley face and texted that she could get a jump on some of the other jobs she had lined up.

Not one of his texts had been personal. It was as if they had nothing to say. Maybe they didn't, but she hated this feeling of unfinished business.

He'd given her a Christmas bonus by sending it along with Jamie. Generous to a fault. And kind. Max knew she'd need extra cash for Christmas.

Taylor and Brody missed him and his girls, but this clean break was for the best. She just wished it didn't hurt so much.

Funny, though, that it didn't feel the same as when Connor had walked out. Then, she'd been scared to be alone, afraid of losing her mother, terrified that she'd mess up badly with two babies at once. But she hadn't been heart broken.

Not like this. She'd developed a habit of rubbing her chest whenever she thought of Max. The boys had learned to hug her when they saw the motion.

They'd stopped asking after the girls and Max a few days back when she'd yelled at them to quit saying their names. She still felt the guilt of that one. *Bad mommy.*

She decided today to make it up to them, by bringing them to the local Christmas tree farm not far from Mrs. Bowler's dog rescue. She grimaced at the lie as she thought it. It hadn't been her idea to come here, it had been Candace's. Kaylin had been pathetically grateful when she'd heard the suggestion. And she suspected Candace was trying to force some Christmas spirit into her broken heart.

Dayna had needed to go to the bathroom so, for the moment, Kaylin was free to let her inner Scrooge mess with her mind. She wanted Christmas to be over. She wanted this false cheer to turn real, but she didn't know how to get there from here.

And she was too weary to try. The happy sounds from the other rows of trees felt like daggers in her ears.

This Christmas tree farm was busy. They were in the row with the shortest, least expensive, trees because she didn't have a lot of ornaments and she wanted the tree to look fully decorated. When Candace had invited her to come along, Kaylin had adjusted her budget to include a real tree for the first time. Her old fake one had become ragged over the years and this would be a treat.

From the next row over came a voice. "Why do *you* think Dad has stopped seeing Kaylin?" It was Lily's voice and she sounded strident, as if she'd asked the question too many times. "Doesn't she like us?"

"Sure, she likes us. We're plenty likable."

Kaylin's heart did an extra beat and she rubbed her chest, feeling the pang of remorse. She bit her lip. She hadn't considered how Max's daughters would feel with the sudden cooling between her and their dad. Of course, she liked them. She'd liked Max's daughters from their first meeting. And the boys...the boys! *Where were they?*

She'd turned her thoughts inward for one minute and off the boys had scampered. How did they know when she was distracted? They must have been born with some kind of radar...

She whirled and saw them playing chase farther along the row. If she stayed where she was, Max's girls would see her. Kaylin rushed toward her sons, shushing them as she went. They giggled and raced each other along the row away from her. Taylor looked over his shoulder, spied her and, naturally, jumped into the next row to hide.

Of course, he chose to hide in the row where Willow and Lily were. *Could she never catch a break?*

Chapter Twenty-one

"Kaylin?" Max's voice carried to her in the crisp winter air and her heart cracked at the sound. Tempted to pretend she didn't hear him Kaylin slowly drew to a halt. She glanced back over her shoulder at Max who stood with Lily and Willow, looking at her. His eyes raked her face, down her body and back to her face.

She closed her eyes so he wouldn't see the yearning she felt. She blinked open again and he was still staring, still dear, still Max. "Hi," she said.

Two squealing boys barrelled past her and straight into the arms of the girls. They staggered under the onslaught, but Willow grabbed up Taylor and Lily hugged Brody as if she'd never let him go.

It hurt, seeing them like this. The obvious affection between the children was poignant as she considered pulling them apart.

Instead of causing a calamity of wails, Kaylin gave Max a half-hearted wave of her gloved hand.

And then Max moved.

Oh, heavens! Max walked with determined strides toward her. As he drew near, she saw, and reacted to, the focus a man gives a woman he wants.

His lips lifted in a lopsided smile as he set his hands on her elbows. Their breaths, soft puffs of white air, mingled between them as Max tilted his head down. "I've missed you," he said. "So much."

"We're here to get a Christmas tree," she murmured. "That's all. Candace invited us." But her heart wasn't in the dismissal and Max's lips turned up at the corner as he recognized the lie for what it was.

"We're back and ready to find the perfect tree," Candace said from behind her. "Oh! Sorry, I didn't mean to interrupt. I'll get the boys out of here."

"No need, they're with my girls," Max said. "Where they belong." His eyes darkened as he gazed at her. Kaylin had never felt so wanted. Had never felt such want. She shivered in reaction, unsure where this conversation would lead, but wanting, badly, to follow it to the end.

"Dayna, we need to get to Taylor and Brody."

"But I wanna find a pretty tree. The best one!" Her sweet voice rose in the cold air, sharp and clear.

"We'll find the boys first. Now, move." Candace's tone brooked no argument.

Kaylin took a deep breath and gave Max a shaky smile.

Candace murmured in Kaylin's ear. "You two take all the time you want to...whatever."

The sound of retreating footsteps followed the words and Kaylin stared up into Max's dear handsome face. "My boys belong with your girls?"

"And you belong with me. But we need to clear the air once and for all."

She nodded. "Yes."

"WHEN I MOVED HERE, I decided that when I was ready to date again, I would avoid single moms," Max said, holding nothing back. He needed to explain himself, no matter the cost. "Last year, I had a relationship ruined by a teenager who couldn't accept me."

Behind him, Willow and Lily had met up with Kaylin's friend and her child. For once, the children were not a concern. The sound of childish voices faded away and he had Kaylin's full attention.

He wanted to kiss her so much he ached. But that wouldn't solve anything.

"Oh, I didn't know the boys were a problem for you." She frowned. "I haven't dated since having them. When their father didn't bond with them, I wanted to protect them from another man abandoning them."

He'd thought as much. "I need to explain what happened." He watched her closely, but she looked interested as she tilted her head to listen. "I believed Lindy and I had a chance of making a go of a second marriage for both of us. Then Karyn told me Willow knew Lindy's daughter to be a bully."

Kaylin gasped. "Ouch, that's harsh."

"Yes, it was a shock," he agreed. "I saw for myself that Izzy manipulated her mom with guilt." In retrospect, he was glad things had turned out as they had. "Lindy wanted to be her daughter's best friend and turned a blind eye to the girl's behavior. Apparently, she'd been a bully from kindergarten. Willow had spent those years avoiding her."

"And suddenly her dad is dating this girl's mother?" Kaylin's eyes widened with concern. "What happened?"

"Izzy made it clear I wasn't wanted, not by either of them. I walked away, ended things, and it was the best decision for me and for my daughters."

Here came the hard part. "I realized the other day that once the work on my house was complete, you and I would move into official dating mode. To be brutally honest, I wondered if I was up for that much commitment. I also wondered if a new commitment to you was fair to Willow and Lily, given the changes they've weathered this last year." He sighed and scrubbed his cheeks. "It also wouldn't be fair to you and the boys if I fell short."

"And now?" she asked, her eyes full of doubt. Doubt that shouldn't be there; but was understandable.

"I'm making a mess of this," he said, wishing he could sweep her into a kiss, so she'd feel what he felt. But no, today, in this moment, words needed to outstrip actions.

"I'll be the judge of what constitutes a mess," she said tartly. "I get what you're saying, and I appreciate you telling me about your doubts." She gave him a warm, but unsteady smile. "It's my turn to come clean."

He looked around and another family was hauling a tree along their row toward them. He grabbed her hand and pulled her over to stand beside some larger trees. Here, the tree boughs touched each other like fingertips brushing and he applauded the added privacy.

"My boys are a lot to take on," she said through a frown. "Their own father wants to desert them. They barely know what he looks like anymore."

Max hated hearing this, hated this Connor with all he had. "Kaylin—"

"No, it's my turn now," she said fiercely. "If I don't say it all, I may never get clear of it."

He nodded and went quiet as he watched her inner battle.

WHAT MAX HAD SAID ABOUT this unknown Lindy woman hurting him cut her deeply. A silent rage against this stupid woman swept through her brain, followed quickly by relief. She was glad he'd walked away. "What exactly happened with Lindy and her girl?"

"We were away for our first weekend together, the three of us. I'd rented a cabin near the ocean in a resort. I came out to the kitchen for breakfast and Izzy told me about the other nice guys her mom had gone out with. She explained that once they'd had a weekend away like the one we were having, Lindy moved on to another nice guy. She warned me off and said she was looking out for me."

"What was the point?"

"She wanted me to understand I wasn't as important as I thought I was." He shrugged. "She made the phrase *nice guy* sound like *stupid guy*. When I asked Lindy about what Izzy said she blustered and said if I didn't believe in us then she was gone. Something about the way she said it, her body language, or the way her eyes shifted, maybe, made me believe her daughter. And when I got home that night, I learned about Willow's opinion. I was happy to make tracks."

"But you felt burned."

"Yeah, I felt burned." He made to reach for her, but Kaylin stepped back. "I shouldn't have brought those feelings into what we have," he admitted. He dropped his arms to his side, and she was sorry for that, but she had to push through.

"Maybe not," she allowed. "But I'm guilty of that sin, too. Connor did a number on me over the last three years. He made me feel like a leech, as if our children didn't deserve a good life. I quit my job because my boss went through a divorce and suddenly decided he could pressure me into having sex. Connor blamed me for enticing the guy."

Thunder stole across Max's face. "I'd like to meet this ex of yours."

"No. He's long ago and forgotten."

"What else has he said to make you feel less than who you are?" He kept his tone cool, but beneath his level expression he seethed.

"You want it all?" she asked.

"I want it all."

Kaylin drew in a slow breath. Fair enough, he'd been honest, and she would be, too. "When I told him that I quit my job and why, Conner said I was looking for the next guy to pay for the boys." She shifted and her voice went fierce. "I had to prove to myself that I don't need that kind of help. I returned to Welcome for a fresh start. A reboot for my life. I don't want to be with a man because I'm broke. I *must* be independent." She needed to trust that no matter what, she could provide for her children.

But she didn't want to be alone, either. She wanted Max. She wanted his girls. She wanted her boys to have Max and Willow and Lily. And by extension, his ex-wife, and her new family.

"I had a small family growing up," she explained. "It was me, my mom, and my aunt and uncle. But you come with a full village of people who care about each other. It's overwhelming."

This time, when Max wanted to pull her close, she went. She rested her weary head on his shoulder and listened to his breathing. He cleared his throat.

"Kaylin, I love you. I love Taylor and Brody. I want you all, so much. Sure, I fell into this thing without planning it. We haven't even been out on a real date. But I want to have that. I want the boys to trust me to be there, the way I am for my girls."

She looked up at him. His jaw was bristled, and she wondered if he'd quit shaving. She brushed his cheek to feel if his beard was soft or wiry. "Have you forgotten to shave?"

"I'm not sure. I may change my look. I turn forty soon. I may launch a whole new me." He was smiling as he said it.

She brushed her lips across his, gently, sweetly. "I love the old you," she breathed.

"You do?" His lips pressed her forehead.

"I do." She closed her eyes as her broken heart filled with a new spirit. New hope blossomed in her chest and she thought she heard a tinkling chime in the air.

"You did hear me say I'll be forty soon?" There was a smile in his voice.

"I turned thirty-five last week."

CHRISTMAS DAY

"Are you comfortable in your hotel?" Kaylin asked her aunt and uncle as they walked up to Max's front door. The boys had run ahead to ring the doorbell four hundred and ninety-five times. They loved making Jackson bark and no matter how often they were told to cut it out, they'd laugh and do one more ring. "Boys! Again?" But the door was opening, framing Max, his girls, and the wiggling poodle.

"We're very comfortable," Aunt June replied. "Stop worrying. We're both fine, right, honey?" Her aunt assured and asked at the same time.

"I'm right as rain," Uncle Mack confirmed. "I've embraced my new exercise routine and I feel great. I walk instead of run and June comes with me now."

"Good, we'll walk Jackson later this morning." As a family, she added to herself.

"He's a handsome dog," her uncle said with a chuckle.

After that, it was mayhem with introductions, hugs, and holiday greetings. Max pulled her into his arms for a quick kiss that took her by surprise.

Willow and Lily threw each other know-it-all looks. From what Max had told her they were taking credit for setting their dad up with Kaylin. They'd managed a few real dates in the time since they'd met at the Christmas tree farm and Kaylin couldn't imagine being any happier.

The house on Cross Street was soon filled with smiles and gifts and friendly conversation.

With coffee, hot chocolate, and cookies served, Max drew her aside. "If you think this is busy, wait until Karyn and crew arrive in two hours. They're having brunch with Cade's in-laws and then they're all coming here together. I should have rented chairs."

"We can run to my place for some if that will help." Her rickety old kitchen chairs might do in a pinch.

"Actually, Logan's dropping some off. He's got his furniture in storage and he swears it's no problem to swing by."

"He's a good friend."

Max checked his watch. "He'll be here any minute."

Right on time, the doorbell chimed, and she followed Max to help with the chairs. "Merry Christmas, Logan," she called with everyone else. He passed in a couple of folding chairs from several he had leaning beside the door.

"I've only got a minute to say hi," Logan said with a gleam in his eye.

"What's that look for?" Kaylin asked. She took two more chairs from his hands, while Max stepped out to bring in the rest.

"I thought you might want to know that Denise Jones is back."

"That was fast, I thought she was gone forever," Max said, as he wrestled the chairs inside. "She quit her job and took off."

"Yes, she did. Burned bridges all over town, too. But that's nothing new for Denise." Logan sighed. "That woman's a piece of work."

An opinion shared by most people in Welcome, from what Candace had told Kaylin.

Aunt June stepped up beside Kaylin. "What happened to bring Denise home so soon?"

Logan scrubbed his face. "Seems she fell in love with an Italian from Naples and he took her for every red cent. At least, that's what she's saying." He made a face of mock disbelief.

Aunt June, who never had a bad word to say about anyone, gave a sound of derision. "She's looking for sympathy. I'm not sure how much she'll get, given her reputation around town."

"I'm off, then," Logan said and waved as he stepped out into the waning light.

Kaylin understood how returning to Welcome could be less than easy, but her luck had changed when Max had saved Taylor's life. Look at her now; surrounded by friends and family and with a growing business. She doubted the same would be said for Denise Jones this time next year.

"Dad, it's time to open presents," Lilly said from the living room. "Taylor and Brody are too excited to wait."

"And you're not?" Max teased. "Yes, it's time," he said with a nervous glance at Kaylin.

"What are you up to?" she asked quietly but got no answer because he made busywork with the chairs by setting them around the room.

Curious, she trailed Max into the living room where the girls had stacked their opened gifts along the wall to make room for the new presents that Kaylin had brought. After she and her aunt and uncle piled their gifts under the tree, she perched on the edge of a new sofa while everyone settled. The boys knelt at her feet so she could keep a hand on their shoulders.

Max took a spot in front of the tree, keeping his gaze locked with hers. "There's one very important gift I want to share with Kaylin, Brody, and Taylor before anything else." He handed her a thick manila envelope. "Open it, please."

The legal sized envelope confused her. What gift could possibly require legal documents? She tugged out the papers and read as she pulled. She only got the pages halfway out before she grasped the meaning. Everything inside stilled, even her heart, as she read the words again and again.

"Honey, what is it?" Her aunt coaxed.

She felt the blood drain from her face as she returned to reality. "Oh, Max. Yes, yes, yes!"

Kaylin rose and walked to him. "Yes, you can adopt Taylor and Brody. Yes, we'll be a family."

"I kept thinking of the word stepdad and how much I want to be more than that. I prefer to be Dad. Plain old Dad. These boys feel like mine, why not make it so?"

Taylor and Brody ran to Kaylin and hugged her, confused. Their parents knelt to their level to give them the news. Max started with,

"Taylor do you remember the first time we met? I grabbed you up off the road."

"You saveded me."

"I believe you saved me. I was lonely that day and a bit scared about fixing up this house. I was worried about Willow and Lily and lots of other grown-up stuff. But then I met you, Brody, and your mom and things became good again."

"Okay!"

"Yay!" Brody chimed in. "Where's my present?" he asked and turned away to search the gaily wrapped packages. His brother joined him, oblivious to the smiles and kisses being shared by Kaylin and Max. Her heart soared as she considered their shared future.

The stunned silence was broken by the laughter of children and the congratulations from her aunt and uncle. The sound carried them through the rest of the busy, family-filled day.

LATER THAT NIGHT...

Kaylin's lovely Aunt June and kind-hearted Uncle Mack had taken the boys to their hotel for the night and the girls were with their mom and Cade.

"We're finally alone," Max said as the door closed behind the last of the crowd. Jackson wiggled his way to stand between them. Max flung his arm over Kaylin's shoulder and drew his love into his side.

"I'll talk to Connor about giving up his parental rights," she said on a long breath out.

"Already done," Max admitted. "We talked two days ago. I congratulated him on the new baby, told him who I was, and suddenly I was his new best friend. He's lucky the conversation was on the phone."

"Oh, Max." She held his face between her palms and blessed his lips with a soft kiss.

"There's only one more thing to do."

"What's that?"

But before she could ask any more questions, he dropped to one knee. "Kaylin Simpson, this adoption will work best if we're married. So, please, please marry me."

"I will," she promised, her gaze solemn and joyful at the same time. Then his love took his hand to lead him upstairs. "We're alone and it's time we do what grownups do when they're alone."

"My bedroom's still looking old and shabby."

"I can fix that, don't you worry." And they climbed the stairs into their bright and happy future full of family and love.

As it should be.

The End

THANK YOU SO MUCH FOR reading *Christmas to the Max A Return to Welcome Novel.* This book was never meant to be. But, when I finished my Love at Christmas trilogy, I had a single dad without a love interest. Anyone who reads romance knows we can't have *that.* When Max Whyte needed to move to be near his daughters, there was nowhere else to put him but in my lovely small town of Welcome, WA.

If you love to discover great books by reading reviews, please pay it forward by sharing your thoughts on Christmas to the Max. A review doesn't have to be long, or a retelling of the plot, just a few words on how you felt when you finished. Did you sigh at the end? Feel happy?

For more Christmas books, please check out my contributions to the Dickens romance series, *The Tinsel Tango, The Rumball Rumba,* and *The Winterland Waltz.*

Over 40 romance titles are listed on my website at https://www.bonnieedwards.com/.

Don't miss out!

Visit the website below and you can sign up to receive emails whenever Bonnie Edwards publishes a new book. There's no charge and no obligation.

https://books2read.com/r/B-A-JXD-TUFJB

BOOKS 2 READ

Connecting independent readers to independent writers.

Did you love *Christmas to the Max*? Then you should read *The Tinsel Tango A Dickens Holiday Novella*[1] by Bonnie Edwards!

The Tango, AKA the dance of love...but when the instructor is hiding his true identity, anything goes...

Stressed-out career-obsessed Brenna James is ordered by he boss to relax, recharge, and surround herself with her loving family in Dickens for Christmas. To fill in time, tango lessons seem just the thing to get her mind off her ambitious plans to get a promotion that will increase her stress and work hours.

But is handsome Jett Smith, her tango instructor, the man he says he is? Something about him doesn't add up. His charm is undeniable, and Brenna soon sets aside her questions as she includes Jett in the

1. https://books2read.com/u/b5oRLp

2. https://books2read.com/u/b5oRLp

James family Christmas in Dickens. Tango is, after all, known as the dance of love.

Jett finds the alluring Brenna and her fun-loving family friendly and accepting. As he spends more time with them, his heart becomes full of a season he's never understood. When he finds the person he's covertly searching for, mixed signals and secrets threaten his plans. His hopes for a future with Brenna are in danger. Christmas in Dickens isn't just quaint, it's life-changing...

About the Author

Bonnie Edwards has been published by Kensington Books, Harlequin Books, Carina Press, and more.

With over 40 titles to her credit, her romances have been translated into several languages. Her books are sold worldwide.

Learn about more exciting releases and get a **free** romance by subscribing to her newsletter, **Bonnie's Newsy Bits** through her website.

https://www.bonnieedwards.com/

Cheers and happy reading!

Bonnie Edwards

www.ingramcontent.com/pod-product-compliance
Lightning Source LLC
Chambersburg PA
CBHW020441180626
46812CB00003B/1352